The Legends of Nod

Also by Glenn Slade Clark, Jr.

Cry, Wolf: Shadow of the Werewolf

THE CHRONICLES OF NIGHTFIRE, TEXAS:
The Vampire Murders
The Haunting of Alexas Mansion

The Great Debate

METROGNOMES:
The Demons of the Blood
The Shaman's Apprentice

THE LEGENDS OF NOD:
The Dragons of Nod
All for the Blood of Nightstorm

The Legends of Nod

Book III

Enter: The Wanderer

Being the third volume in the first saga
The Sword of Libran

A story from
The Epic of Prince Joryn

by

Glenn Slade Clark, Jr.

2019

The Legends of Nod, Book III:
Enter: The Wanderer

First Edition: February 2015
Second Edition Hardback: August 2019
Second Edition Trade Paperback: August 2019

Published by Clark Ink, LLC.

Cover art by Molly Fine.

This novella was originally published as
The Legends of Nod #3 "Enter: The Wanderer."

ISBN-13: 978-1-61815-119-3

In memoriam, for the heroic first responders
whom we lost the day the towers fell.

And for those they left behind.

Contents

Dramatis Personae

Operator Golan Binju – Human male from the kingdom of Brethmour, age forty-two years; son of Floran and Emma Binju; brother of Rolu Binju; com screen operator at Palace Nod

Charger – Unicorn male from the Field of Crystal, age 300 years; son of Sir Illium and Lady Norlan; royal steed of Prince Kail

Prince Dorago – Human male from the kingdom of Nod, age twenty-four years; son of Emperor Sapros and Lady Riko; older brother of Princess Enjinia and Princess Lily; younger half-brother of Prince Kail, Prince Repteré, Princess Willowyll, Prince Dakarai, Princess Hero, Prince Mwana, and Princess Adaeze; older half-brother of Prince Vail and Prince Joryn

Dreadfin – Fingrin male from the Reef of Shaard-Amm, age seventy-nine years; servant of the Wanderer

Ambassador Dorran Equus – Centaur male from the nomadic Caluman tribe, age thirty-eight years; son of Rinaulf and Gylanna Equus; widower of Kalibi Equus; father of Lute Equus; ambassador to the Imperial court of Nod, representing the Twelve Tribes of the centaurs; master of hand-to-hand combat; champion of the Caluman tribe; urged by the Lord Caluman to ally himself more closely with his friend, Prince Joryn, after the young prince's successful peace accord with the Empire of Dragons

Lord Galen – Human male from the Imperial colony of the Whispering Plains, age twenty years; son of Lord Pleidies and Lady Galendria; Lord of Ruby Point; paramour of Prince Joryn

Gemina – Human female from the caverns of Mount Wyvrn, age nineteen years; older twin sister of Gemino; sorceress; servant of the Wanderer

Gemino – Human male from the caverns of Mount Wyvrn, age nineteen years; younger twin brother of Gemina; sorcerer; servant of the Wanderer

Princess Hero – Human female from the Kingdom of Nod, age twenty-six years; daughter of Emperor Sapros and Lady Leita; older sister of Prince Vail; younger half-sister of Prince Kail, Prince Repteré, Princess Willowyll, and Prince Dakarai; older half-sister of Prince Mwana, Princess Adaeze, Prince Dorago, Princess Enjinia, Princess Lily, and Prince Joryn

Sir Illium – Bionic unicorn male from the Golden Field, age 1,000 years; son of Ryjan and Maladine; husband of Lady Norlan; father of Charger; knight of the Order of the Golden Field; royal steed of Prince Joryn; recently injured and fitted with bionic prosthetics by Kabed, after being mutilated by the evil demigod Warclaw

Iron Bill – Deluvian war bird male, from the kingdom of Deluvia, age 4,588 years; son of Red Rodger and Dawn Glider; last of the Deluvian war birds; charged by his friend Libran to protect and assist the priestess Tianna

Jakknife – GolemBot Weapon-N Assassin, male gender identity programming, from the city of Mech Valley, age 1,499 years; servant of the Wanderer; formerly known as GB-WNA-666

Guardsman Jesstra – Human male from the Imperial colony of the Whispering Plains, age twenty-two years; son of Rindal and Shey; member of the Imperial Guard, stationed at Palace Nod

Prince Joryn – Human male from the Kingdom of Nod, age twenty years; youngest son of Emperor Sapros and the Unnamed Empress; younger brother of Prince Kail; youngest half-brother of Prince Repteré, Princess Willowyll, Prince Dakarai, Princess Hero, Prince Mwana, Princess Adaeze, Prince Dorago, Princess Enjinia, Prince Vail, and Princess Lily; paramour of Lord Galen; newly appointed champion of Libran; recently returned from a successful peace accord with King Orlok the Unforgiven, after defeating the king's forces at the Battle of Chiroptera

Kabed – Human male from the kingdom of Deluvia, age twenty-four years; tech wizard; Imperial head of science for Emperor Sapros; inventor of the robotic unicorns called Unitrons

Prince Kail – Human male from the Kingdom of Nod, age thirty-five years; eldest son of Emperor Sapros and the Unnamed Empress; older brother of Prince Joryn; eldest half-brother of Prince Repteré, Princess Willowyll, Prince Dakarai, Princess Hero, Prince Mwana, Princess Adaeze, Prince Dorago, Princess Enjinia, Prince Vail, and Princess Lily; husband of Princess Maressah; heir apparent to the thrones of both the Kingdom of Nod and the Empire of Nod; member of Emperor Sapros' Advisory Council

Lowgun Kin – Reptisaur male from the city of Slythe Orn, age 102 years; professional speedracer; owner of the *Dragon Racer*; outlaw, wanted dead or alive by the Mech Valley Authority; encouraged by Libran, along with his friends, Longshot and Trig, to join the cause of Prince Joryn at the Battle of Chiroptera in order to help turn the tide in favor of the Imperial army

Lance – Unitron (robotic unicorn), male gender identity programming, from the Kingdom of Nod, age two weeks; unofficial steed of Prince Vail; also known as Unitron 003

Longshot – Human male from the city of TexStar, age nineteen years; paramour of Princess Pumpkitina; gunslinger; outlaw, wanted dead or alive by the Mech Valley Authority; encouraged by Libran, along with his friends, Lowgun Kin and Trig, to join the cause of Prince Joryn at the Battle of Chiroptera in order to help turn the tide in favor of the Imperial army; hopeful that Joryn and his band of heroes will return the favor by helping him rescue Princess Pumpkitina from the robotic despot of Mech Valley, Torakku N'obotto

Princess Maressah – Human female from the kingdom of Aise, age thirty-four years; daughter of King Willfriez and Queen Mistrie; wife of Prince Kail

Lieutenant Moon – Human male from the city of Bluepearl, age twenty-seven years; son of Ritson and Lani; younger brother of Kaliope; older brother of Bander; second-in-command of the Imperial Guard, stationed at Palace Nod

Guardsman Pim – Human male from the fallen city of Brookdale, age twenty-one years; son of Rip and Dania; member of the Imperial Guard, stationed at Palace Nod

(Miiko) Quickwing – Celestian male from the kingdom of Celestia, age twenty-eight years; son of Strongtide and Starsong; master of the broadsword; champion of the kingdom of Celestia; tasked by his uncle, Chief Sunray, to serve at the side of Prince Joryn; recently wounded at the Battle of Chiroptera while rescuing Prince Joryn from an enemy blade

General Razorwing – Chirop male from the kingdom of Chiroptera, age fifty-three years; son of Ranshaarr and Aelbludd; general over the forces of the Wanderer; formerly known as Nightstorm the Merciless

Prince Repteré – Human male from the Kingdom of Nod, age thirty years; son of Emperor Sapros and Lady Makhaira; older brother of Princess Willowyll, younger half-brother of Prince Kail; older half-brother of Prince Dakarai, Princess Hero, Prince Mwana, Princess Adaeze, Prince Dorago, Princess Enjinia, Prince Vail, Princess Lily, and Prince Joryn

Emperor Sapros – Human male from the Kingdom of Nod, age sixty years; son of Emperor Barnard and Imperial Queen Mother Mideerma; older brother of Prince Bohmaine; widower of the Unnamed Empress; husband of Lady Makhaira, Lady Amina, Lady Leita, and Lady Riko; father of Prince Kail, Prince Repteré, Princess Willowyll, Prince Dakarai, Princess Hero, Prince Mwana, Princess Adaeze, Prince Dorago, Princess Enjinia, Prince Vail, Princess Lily, and Prince Joryn; ruler of both the Kingdom of Nod and the Empire of Nod

Drae Shivvan – Highland Elf male from the kingdom of the Highlands, age twenty-seven years; son of Burcher and Linelle Shivvan; older brother of Lin Shivvan; champion of the Highlands; recently cursed by the Mark of Centaurus, after betraying the eponymous god's plan to have Prince Joryn killed at the Battle of Chiroptera; having joined the ranks of Joryn's elite thereafter, his body continues to be slowly consumed by Centaurus' curse

Onri Sprigg – Lowland Elf male from Candy Village, age thirty-five years; son of Pipper and Nesta Sprigg; younger brother of Lesha Garmen and Kirna Figg; older brother of Zazu Sprigg; famous adventurer and swordsman; champion of the kingdom of the Lowlands; Onri's exploits in the Outer World have been famously chronicled in a trilogy of books by the renowned Lowland scribe Dandy Jim; tasked by Governor Bumble Pepper to serve at the side of Prince Joryn

Captain Starro – Human male from the kingdom of Nod, age twenty-nine years; son of Fenjian and Raya; older brother of Killian, Arrie, and Lanzer; Captain of the Imperial Guard, stationed at Palace Nod

Priestess Tianna – Human female, age nineteen years; priestess of the Temple of Libran on the grounds of Palace Nod; trained as an empath and mystic healer; possessed of mysterious powers that she is only just beginning to unlock within herself, including the ability to mystically summon and bind the so-called gods, as she did to Centaurus, helping her to uncover his sinister plot against Joryn during the Battle of Chiroptera

Trig – Robotic horse/light gun, male gender identity programming, from the city of Mech Valley, age five years; steed of Longshot; outlaw, wanted decommissioned by the Mech Valley Authority; encouraged by Libran, along with his friends, Longshot and Lowgun Kin, to join the cause of Prince Joryn at the Battle of Chiroptera in order to help turn the tide in favor of the Imperial army

Prince Vail – Human male from the Kingdom of Nod, age twenty-two years; son of Emperor Sapros and Lady Leita; younger brother of Princess Hero; younger half-brother of Prince Kail, Prince Repteré, Princess Willowyll, Prince Dakarai, Prince Mwana, Princess Adaeze, Prince Dorago, and Princess Enjinia; older half-brother of Princess Lily, and Prince Joryn

The Wanderer – Widely believed to be the first human in Nod, though tales of his origin and history are often contrary; Lord of Mount Dread; holds aspirations of universal conquest, focused on the Empire of Nod

Warclaw – Mutant human demigod male (has the appearance of a human/crab hybrid), age nineteen years; son of the goddess Cancerelle; servant of the Wanderer; has recently bested Prince Joryn and Sir Illium in battle twice, rending Illium's body and leaving him for dead both times

Princess Willowyll – Human female from the kingdom of Nod, age twenty-nine years; daughter of Emperor Sapros and Lady Makhaira; younger sister of Prince Repteré; younger half-sister of Prince Kail; older half-sister of Prince Dakarai, Princess Hero, Prince Mwana, Princess Adaeze, Prince Dorago, Princess Enjinia, Prince Vail, Princess Lily, and Prince Joryn

The Legends of Nod

Book III

Enter: The Wanderer

Chapter 1: Quickwing's Return

"Joryn! I was hoping it was you." Galen smiled from the wall screen in Joryn's room, his image projected from his own room in Pleidies Tower at the heart of the Whispering Plains.

Joryn beamed. "I miss you so much, Galen. It's been agony not seeing you in person. I had wanted to come sooner, but that crisis in Chiroptera threw everything off."

"I know, Joryn. Not to worry. I have infinite patience." Galen rolled his eyes, playfully. "So is there news then? Do you know when you'll be arriving?"

Joryn sighed and leaned back on his bed. "Not yet, but today is the day that Father is meeting with his Advisory Council. I had submitted my requests in writing the day after my return, but I haven't even seen him since then. We didn't part company on the best of terms. I'm hoping Kail was right, that he'll be more than willing to have me out of the palace for a little while. He's certainly made no secret of avoiding me for the past ten days."

"I hope Kail's right too," Galen agreed. "In fact, I'd bet good money that he is. Hell, if you were my kid, I'd toss you out on your arrogant hide right now." He laughed. "So, what do you think? Another week?"

"At worst," Joryn said. "You know I'd leave for the Whispering Plains the very instant Father granted permission, if not for my debt to Longshot."

"I bear him no ill will on that account," Galen said. "He did contribute tremendously to getting you back home from Chiroptera alive." He eyed the two pistols hanging on his own wall with a sly smile. "I think I'd like to test his skills, if ever I meet him. I'm intrigued by what you've told me."

Joryn shook his head. "Even with his magnificent shape-changing steed, he'd be no match for you. How many trophies have you won for your sharpshooting now, anyway?"

Galen shrugged. "Who's counting?"

"Anyway, Father will make his decision in council, and then, if he agrees to both requests, I'll be off with my men to save Longshot's girlfriend from this Torakku N'obotto character. Would it sound arrogant if I said I thought it would take a day?"

"Yes," Galen said. "But I find self-confidence attractive, so by all means carry on."

"I don't know." Joryn shrugged. "I'm not as conceited as it may sound. It's just that, compared to what happened in Chiroptera, a rescue mission sounds … easy."

"It's all about perspective, man," Galen said.

"However it goes, I'll be coming to the Whispering Plains just as soon as I get back from Mech Valley. We'll set out first thing tomorrow, if it goes our way with the Advisory Council."

"It will." Galen winked with certainty. "So, did the Fighter Discs my father sent arrive without a hitch?"

"Yes," Joryn said. "We are very grateful for the gift! I am only sorry that you couldn't make the delivery in person."

"Yeah, me too," Galen said. "But my aunt and my cousin Everron are visiting, and my first duty here is to be their gracious host. It's not a bad thing. Everron and I have been like brothers since we were children. I just would rather be with you right now."

A red light started blinking at the bottom right corner of Joryn's screen.

"Hold on," Joryn said. "I have another call. Could be something official."

"Like I said," Galen shrugged, "infinite patience here, man."

Joryn hit the red light, and Galen's image was replaced by that of the diminutive Lowland Elf Onri Sprigg. "My prince."

"Sprigg! What can I do for you, my friend?"

"I thought you'd want to know, Quickwing has returned from Celestia."

"That's fantastic! I didn't think he'd be back so soon."

"Neither did he," Onri assured him. "And he's pouting so hard I thought he might trip over his lips on the way to his quarters. He's acting like a small baby whose mother replaced her nursing chocolate with fish eggs."

"Nursing choco—?" Joryn shook his head. "Never mind." He smiled. "I'll be down to see him at once."

Onri nodded and broke the connection.

Galen's face immediately returned to the screen. "Well?"

"My friend Quickwing, the Celestian who was wounded at Chiroptera, has returned. I need to go and welcome him back home."

Galen nodded, wondering quietly at the idea of having Joryn welcome *him* home someday. "Go to it then, my prince."

"We'll see each other soon," Joryn assured him.

"Infinite patience."

"I know. I love you."

Galen winked. "You should."

Joryn knocked on the door to Quickwing's quarters. When there was no answer, he said, "Quickwing, it's me, Joryn. May I come in?"

"Come," answered the Celestian somberly.

Joryn opened the door and entered, finding the dark room sparsely lit by only a few candles. He found Quickwing sitting up straight on the bed, his legs crossed, wings folded behind him, hands palm upward and resting on his knees, eyes closed.

"Have I come at a bad time?" the prince asked.

Quickwing opened his eyes and looked to the young human. "No better or worse than any other. How may I be of service?"

Joryn smiled. "I just wanted to see how you have recovered from the battle. We've all been awaiting your return eagerly."

"I'm sorry for the state of it then. I'm sorry to disappoint you, my prince."

Joryn laughed. "Disappoint me? Quickwing, you saved my life! I cannot put into words my joy at your healthy return."

"I cannot fly," Quickwing said flatly, sadness evident in the timbre of his voice. "I am of no use to anyone in this state."

Joryn was stunned. "Cannot fly? How can that be?"

"I needed more time to heal. I didn't want to come back like this; to be shamed in the presence of Nod's great warriors. But Chief Sunray insisted I tarry no longer in Celestia. He wants me here to represent our people in your band of warrior elites. But I am no longer 'elite.' " He repeated with a shake of his head, "I cannot fly."

"But there's no shame at all, Quickwing," Joryn protested. "You're a hero, a great warrior. How many times can I say that you saved my life before you'll hear it? None of the rest of us can fly either, my friend. Besides, I'm sure it isn't permanent. Your wings weren't even wounded, were they? What happened?"

"My chest is still healing. It is stitched. I cannot flap my wings, or I'll burst the stitches; open the wound. They come out in a week or two, but until then, I am a waste of space. I am ashamed to be in the company of your elite, when I can offer nothing."

"Quickwing," Joryn said earnestly, "your being here, returned to us and on the healing path, is a tremendous gift to me. There is great value in it. It gives us all joy and hope. And there are none among us who do not recall the courage with which you received your wound. You are a hero among heroes."

"You sound like my uncle, the chief. I thought he was encouraging me to leave so soon, because he wanted me out of his sight, though he said similar things to what you say now. He said he was proud of me, that he wanted me at Palace Nod to represent us. I was sure he was just saying things to get me to go, and then he ordered it. I can't see what you have to gain from comforting me, so I suppose I must accept your words as genuine. But … I still don't feel very much like a hero, my prince."

"Call me Joryn. We are friends, Quickwing." The prince smiled warmly.

The Celestian turned and regarded the young man, a genuine smile on his own lips for the first time since he had returned. "And you, Joryn, must call me Miiko."

"But that's your—"

"Yes, it is my heart name, given to me by my mother. It is a name only permitted to be used by family and my closest friends, and it would greatly honor me if you would count yourself among my closest friends, Joryn; if you would call me by my heart name."

"Miiko," Joryn said, "the honor is mine."

Miiko nodded, pleased at the sound of his less formal name coming from the prince's lips.

"Now," Joryn ventured, "would you consider seeing Tianna about your wound? She may have some mystical way to speed along the healing."

"I will, my friend. Just leave me to my meditations a little while longer."

Joryn nodded. "Of course. And, Miiko," he added, before leaving the warrior to his candle-lit solitude, "welcome home."

Joryn left, the door closing behind him, and Quickwing closed his eyes, returning all of his energy to the meditation of his deepest inner sorrows.

Chapter 2: The King's Council

"And lastly," King Sapros said, having already lorded over a lengthy meeting with his council of twelve advisors, "there is the matter of my youngest son's desires to travel to Mech Valley to aid in the rescue of Princess Pumpkitina, which he hopes to follow with a personal journey to the Whispering Plains, to spend time with his paramour." The king sighed, weary from it all, and rubbed his forehead. "I see no reason not to grant his requests, but I am open to your thoughts. Is there anything we may ask him to gain for us that we have not considered, while he is abroad? Is there anything we might lose for allowing it? Speak."

The only prince to sit on the Advisory Council, the king's eldest son Kail, spoke up encouragingly, addressing his fellows. "I agree with my father. I see no reason not to grant my brother's requests. We will surely gain an ally in the queen of Pumpkin Land, when her daughter is safely returned to her, and we will only reinforce the loyalty of Lord Pleidies and the people of our colony in the Whispering Plains by embracing his son's relationship with Nod's great hero."

The king nodded, though his face showed a nauseous reaction to the mention of his youngest son's now legendary heroism.

"Are you sure that Pumpkin Land is the *right* sort of alliance for us to be forging, my prince?" Drokkus, a harsh member of the council, concerned more with profits and power than with the welfare of the people, addressed the prince rather than the king, in an effort to avoid appearing to question his sovereign. "Why waste the time and resources to send our new poster boy in to rescue some minor princess from, let's face the facts, the Wyyrd Outback. These aren't the sorts of kingdoms we want falling in with the Empire of Nod. They're too peculiar and not nearly powerful enough to matter."

The elderly philosopher, Parakletos, who had tutored both Kail and Joryn throughout their youth, spoke up in the plan's defense. "Are there really such things as 'wrong sorts' of people in need, Drokkus? Surely the goal of any *just* empire should be to promote harmony among *all* peoples. And one never knows when a *peculiar* alliance may be just the sort we need. I must stand with my prince *and* my emperor on this matter. Sending Joryn and his elite into the Wyyrd Outback is just and worthwhile. Not to mention the debt the Empire owes to Longshot, Trig, and

Lowgun for coming to our aid during the Battle of Chiroptera. Longshot personally stormed the throne room of King Orlok with our prince. How ungrateful we would seem, if we should deny his request for aid."

Kail nodded his agreement, then added, "And the resources we spend will be minimal. It is a small operation compared to the Chiropteran problem. We are sending in and supplying just a handful of warriors, not an army. For an imperial budget, this is next to nothing, a tiny droplet pulled from a vast ocean of wealth."

Drokkus grumbled, his thick, black eyebrows turning down profoundly. Silently conceding the matter, he moved to the next. "But on to the matter of this *personal* visit to the Whispering Plains; I do see a clear loss to the Empire in allowing it."

"How so?" asked Emperor Sapros, curious.

"My king, if I may say so, there is a great resource that has long gone ignored, which perhaps the time has come to put to greater use."

"I'm listening," Sapros said calmly.

"Your children, sire. Your *unmarried* children. These are no mere citizens of Nod, free to choose their pairings at their leisure. Their coupling off should *benefit* the Empire. I fear this match that Prince Joryn has made with the son of Lord Pleidies is folly. Lord Pleidies' loyalty is already secure. He governs an Imperial colony and is *well* compensated with lands and wealth of his own. Joryn could be matched with a more lucrative mate, perhaps one with whom he might further seal an alliance, with *children.* Surely the fact that there will be no heirs to this union between the

House of Sapros and the House of Pleidies is reason enough to discourage it.

"Much as the dalliance of your son Prince Vail with that wood nymph Merridy should be discouraged. I know he has not proclaimed anything serious, but he has written songs about her and goes to the forest often to visit with her. She's an immortal, a tree spirit. There is nothing to be gained for the Empire in this childish flirtation."

Many heads nodded in agreement with Drokkus.

The king himself had grown progressively more uncomfortable in appearance as Drokkus had moved from the matter of Joryn and Galen to the matter of Vail and the immortal Merridy. "Is everyone in agreement on this?" Sapros asked, ignoring his obvious distaste for the subject.

"No!" Kail shouted. "Listen to yourselves! How does forcing our princes to have less than human hearts endear us to the people of Nod? Joryn and Vail are heroes. They are names and faces that are much loved by the people. Would it not sour the hearts of the citizens towards their emperor, if he were to tear these young *heroes* away from their loves?

"And in the case of Joryn and Galen, it is already a matter of great pride to the Plains colonists that their young lord is the chosen paramour of the emperor's son who brought peace with the dragons of Din *and* the bat folk of Chiroptera. He is *their* hero, and he has shown them *great* favoritism in his love for Galen. Would you now have our emperor strip that pride away from them in order to give it to some less loyal kingdom or tribe? Would you turn their hearts against the king for this, when there are so many other children he has had who may deliver you with what you might say were more suitable pairings in time?"

"Indeed," Parakletos chimed in. "I agree that Joryn and Galen present an untouchable political connection. With Joryn's fame on the rise, we must be careful not to turn his followers against the emperor. There is nothing harmful in this coupling with Lord Galen, and the people enjoy seeing their hero happy. I would say, let us keep our hands off of Prince Joryn, watch, and see what other alliances he forges for us *without* being betrothed. Surely he did not need to *marry* a dragon or a Chirop to bring them into our circle of friends."

Drokkus was not swayed by these arguments. "It is a *waste* to show favoritism to a realm as small and far from imposing as the Whispering Plains. The cost of their pride over Joryn's choice is nothing compared to the gain of pairing Joryn with someone more powerful, someone with resources they can share to the greater benefit of our own kingdom."

Parakletos cleared his throat, an affectation that he favored over raising his voice when things became heated. "I must remind you, Drokkus, of the gift we received from the Whispering Plains just yesterday, in the form of ten of their remarkable flying Fighter Discs. Are we not *already* seeing a benefit to the capital kingdom as a result of Joryn's choice in lovers?"

"Yes," Drokkus spat, "but what *else* do they have to give? Surely we now have all they can possibly offer us, and the profits to be had from this potential union dried up the very instant after we received the Fighter Discs."

"I agree with Parakletos and my son," Sapros said, ending the debate. "We will not touch Joryn." He considered. "For now."

"Your wisdom is great, my king," offered Drokkus obsequiously. "Would you then consider, perhaps, finding suitable spouses for your other offspring?"

"This has come up before," Sapros grumbled. "I have held off on their marriages in order to forge alliances through them in the future. We have simply had no need."

"I agree wholeheartedly with the wisdom in this," Drokkus assured him. "I would only suggest that, perhaps, now might be a good time to offer these young nobles as a demonstration of goodwill towards a kingdom already under the Empire's banner. Why should the Whispering Plains be the only country so honored? Are there not other kingdoms who have given you more, who wield more power; who are far more *worthy* of the affections of your children?"

Prince Kail spoke up, finding himself ever opposed to the recommendations of Drokkus, "I see the fact that we have no *need* of using them to expand the borders of the Empire with alliances as proof enough that they should be allowed to choose partners of their own. After all, I chose *my* own wife. Why send my sisters and brothers into misery when it is not necessary?"

"You are too soft-hearted, my prince," Drokkus said with theatrical pity. "Yours is an *Imperial* family. I'm afraid that politics must reign in place of love. Everything the Empire gives must have a return that is greater in value. Even the marriages of its princes and princesses."

The king cleared his throat. "You both make valid points. I agree there is no *need* to marry off my sons and daughters, as far as forging new alliances at present. However, the pairing of Joryn and Galen *has* given undue honor to the Whispering Plains. Rather than vilify myself by stripping them of that honor, I suggest we start looking at suitable husbands for my daughters from other kingdoms within the Empire. Kingdoms with more to give us in return."

He looked to his son. "Your sisters will be permitted to make their own choices, of course, as there is no urgency in the matter, but we will *encourage* them when it comes to narrowing down their selections."

He looked back to Drokkus. "We will begin with the courtship of Princess Willowyll." He took in the whole council with his eyes. "I will hear suggestions, next week, from this council, on potential suitors."

To Kail, he said, "Give Vail the message that I am not amused over this nonsense with the wood nymph. It must end, and it must end now.

"And tell Joryn that he has leave to go on this mission to the Wyyrd Outback, after which, he may go to the Whispering Plains for one week."

"Only a week?" Kail asked.

"Did I stammer, boy? We will indulge his heart's desire, but we mustn't have him getting too familiar with the people of the Plains. He is an Imperial prince and must remain, in their eyes, to a great degree, superior."

Sapros slammed a mallet down on the great oak table, ending the meeting. He stood to leave, and when he had gone, the council members followed suit.

CHAPTER 3:
WAR WOUNDS

"YOU'VE LOST TEN POUNDS SINCE I SAW YOU LAST week." Tianna regarded Drae Shivvan, who had come for her aid in the Temple of Libran once again.

"It doesn't matter," Drae said through clenched teeth. "It's the pain, Priestess. It's slowly destroying me. Can you stop the pain again?" There were tears in his eyes, as he held a hand tightly over the burning Mark of Centaurus on his flesh; the god whom he had betrayed at the Battle of Chiroptera.

Tianna nodded, feeling pity for the once proud warrior of the Highland Elves. She turned to go to her cupboard, and she spoke, as she removed a jar and began counting out pills into a pouch. "Have you gone through all of the pills I gave you last week already?"

"I have."

She prepared a glass of water, and she took him a pill in the palm of her hand, along with the pouch filled with pills for later use. She handed him the stray pill and the glass of water. "This mark is consuming you, Drae."

"I know it." He winced, as he removed his hand from the mark long enough to swallow the pill with a gulp of water. "I will hold out as long as I can. Meanwhile, these pills have helped."

Tianna shook her head, regretfully. "I'm still trying to find a more long-term solution for this, but it's not easy fighting the magic of a Guardian."

"A what?"

"A god," Tianna amended. "I am not a servant of Centaurus, nor am I on good terms with him, after Chiroptera. Perhaps, if I were among *his* clergy, or if I had the ear of the high priest of Nod, I would be able to find a solution; but I fear if you go into one of Centaurus' temples for aid, you will only find destruction, and I promise you, if I were to consult the high priest on this matter, he would only have me send you to them for punishment. Gods have forever to hold a grudge, but they tend to deal with those who betray them rather quickly."

"Then why do I live still?"

"The tone in your voice gives it away, Drae. It's clear that this pain has made you see death as a mercy. Centaurus wants you to suffer. So I will keep trying to end your suffering. Meantime, these pills are all you have, and they are made from Spiritwood fruit, which is not easy to come by. I've asked Vail to bring back some more at his next opportunity. But still, take these sparingly, only when the pain is at its worst. We need to make them last."

Drae nodded, his muscles relaxing. "I feel better already. I do not deserve your kindness, Priestess."

"Joryn forgave you. That's good enough for me."

"How many know?"

"About your deception, you mean?"

Drae nodded miserably.

"No one has shared the tale who knows it. Just me, Bill, Joryn, Onri, and Kabed."

"That's quite enough to hate myself over."

"Hate yourself for the deed," Iron Bill chimed in from the rafters, "not for its discovery."

Drae looked up to the metallic war bird, wounded by the words.

Tianna glared at Iron Bill and hurriedly tried to smooth things over. "Bill means no harm, Drae. He has a tendency to quote ancient philosophical aphorisms. He's very old."

Bill simply huffed and held his tongue.

Drae nodded, not believing Tianna's explanation, but accepting it as a courtesy.

A shadow fell over them, and they turned to see the brawny form of Quickwing coming in through the front of the temple. Drae went pale at the sight of the bandage across the Celestian's muscular chest, recalling in vivid detail his own actions that had led to the warrior taking a blade for Prince Joryn.

Quickwing, entirely unaware that Drae had any feelings of guilt over his injury, still regarded the other warrior uncomfortably, feeling unworthy to be counted in his company. "I'm sorry. If I'm interrupting, I can come back later."

"No," Drae said quickly. "I'm finished here." He nodded to the priestess, "Thank you for the medicine," and he walked quickly down the aisle and out of the temple without another word.

Quickwing looked down, not meeting the priestess' eyes. "He despises me, as I despise myself."

Tianna actually giggled at the Celestian's self-deprecation. "Why would he not love you, Quickwing?"

"It's what I'm here to discuss with you, at Joryn's urging. This wound on my chest. I'm no warrior until it is healed. I cannot fly. I am of no value, lame, a burden. One such as Drae Shivvan must surely detest such weakness."

"Perhaps you project your own feelings too liberally, mighty hero," Iron Bill said.

"Ah, but perhaps not," Quickwing countered, looking up to the bird. "Where would you have been without your wings in the recent battle? Where would I be, had you not helped to fly me home after I fell?"

Bill said nothing.

"How can I help you, Quickwing?" Tianna asked.

"Joryn thought, perhaps, you might have some way to speed along my healing, in addition to the attention I'll be receiving from the palace physicians."

"The wound is deep," she answered. "I am not an expert on biological medicines, nor on physical wounds such as yours. But I can lay hands over you, to sooth you, as it heals. I cannot speed things along though. I'm afraid you're fully in the hands of your physicians."

"I see." He looked even more downcast. "Joryn will be disappointed."

"Only for your sake, Quickwing," the priestess added. "I assure you, he is pleased to have you back at the palace, top condition or not. I have known him a long time. As for you, you must allow yourself to be wounded, before you can allow yourself to heal. Be patient. Let me sooth you as well as I can."

"I suppose soothing is better than nothing. I accept your kind offer, Priestess."

"Good," She said with an amused smile. "Now come this way."

Chapter 4: Captain Starro's Secret

In the courtyard of Palace Nod, a demonstration was taking place. "Now, hold still, Captain."

Captain Starro of the Imperial Guard grimaced. "I will, Kabed. Even more so if you kill me."

Kabed laughed and took aim, squinting one eye shut. "You won't die, Captain. That's the point." He fired the dart from the pistol in his hand, and it sailed through the air with a whistle.

Captain Starro opened his mouth to further voice his doubts but was knocked in the chest by the dart before he could utter a word. The dart stuck to his armor through an adhesive, and ropes of quick-drying glue shot out of compartments on the sides of the dart instantly, wrapping around the captain and binding his arms to his sides and his legs to each other. "Kabed …" Starro wobbled in place for a moment, then quickly lost his balance and fell to the ground. "Okay. It works."

"And …?"

"And I'm not dead. Now cut me loose, you mad tech wizard."

Joryn, Longshot, and Lowgun clapped their hands, Longshot hooting his approval. The mechanical horse Trig whinnied with amusement, and the grand old unicorn Illium smiled with his twinkling eyes but said nothing aloud.

"Quite an invention, Kabed," Joryn said. "What do you call it?"

Kabed, who had knelt down to cut the captain of the Guard free from the bonds, shrugged. "I don't know. Capture Dart? Glue Gun? I'm not there yet."

Onri Sprigg approached the group, assessing the situation, as Kabed's knife broke the bonds, and Captain Starro got back to his feet none the worse for wear, thanks to his armor and generally unflappable nature. "I suggest calling it the Glueteus Maximus. A fine, elegant name for such a device," the elf said.

Joryn and Longshot snickered.

Kabed picked up the dart. "Yes, well, you know how I value your input on these things, Sprigg," he offered sarcastically.

"Hm. And well you should. Have you read my trilogy yet?"

"Um … Not yet," Kabed confessed. "I'll get to it."

"See that you do!" The diminutive warrior turned to the others. "So, what's everyone doing?"

"Waiting on word from the Council," Joryn answered. "If they give their approval, we will begin preparations to leave for Mech Valley, to help Longshot save his girlfriend."

"Meanwhile," Longshot added, "we're watching Kabed knock Captain Starro on his butt. How did he talk you into bein' a test dummy anyway, buddy?"

"To tell the truth," Starro answered, "I lost a bet."

"That you did," Kabed agreed with all possible smugness.

"What kind of bet?" Joryn asked.

"It had to do with three Diamoonian dancing girls and Kabed's alleged ability to woo them."

Kabed held up a finger in mock sternness. "Never doubt the limitless powers of my charm, Starro."

Joryn laughed. "So, you two were making a night of it then?"

"He was," Starro answered. "I was simply making an appearance in town on my night off. Good for the Guard to see me letting off some steam. It gives them silent permission to do the same."

"So?" Longshot nudged the guardsman teasingly. "How many dancing girls did *you* lasso, Captain?"

"None, Longshot. I was only there to make an appearance."

"And to volunteer to test my new Trapper Dart!" Kabed added. "No. Rocket Net?" He shook his head. "Still getting there."

"Aw," Longshot said. "What's the matter, Cap? You married or somethin'?"

"No, no," Starro answered uncomfortably. He turned to Joryn, changing the subject as rapidly as he could. "Forgive me, my prince, but I have not had time to congratulate you on your victory at Chiroptera since your return. My duties at the palace kept me from joining you, I'm afraid, but I heard all about it from Lieutenant Moon. I was highly, *highly* impressed. Who'd have believed such a battle could be won without a single life lost? In fact, I'm putting in a request to your father to have the Guard switch to light guns that only work on stun, to honor your methods."

"I am honored indeed, Captain," Joryn beamed. It was nice, after all of the struggle to get anyone to see the merits of his plan, to finally have the validation of a renowned man of arms.

"And now, if you'll all excuse me," Starro bowed his head to Joryn, "I have a personal matter to attend to."

"Off you go then, Captain," Joryn said with a laugh.

Starro turned to Kabed. "And if you need any more test dummies, I'll be sure to send one of my men."

Kabed laughed at the young captain and offered a jocose salute.

As Captain Starro walked away, Longshot asked, "So, he's really *not* married?"

"I thought you had a girlfriend, who we are all going to ride off to rescue," Kabed said.

Lowgun laughed under his breath.

"What're you laughin' at, scale face?" Longshot asked.

"Oh, nothing, sidekick," the lizard man said. "I was just thinking of your tendency to flirt with anything that speaks. You could give Kabed a run for his money in the taverns, that I know for sure."

"Shut up, bug breath! I'm not *that* easy! Never hit on you, did I? And you're *my* sidekick, remember, not the other way around!

Besides, I love Pumpkitina. Really, I do. I was just wondering why Starro wouldn't have been into Diamoonian dancing girls is all. They're *quite* appealing to most of us humanoids."

Onri shrugged. "Maybe it's the sharp edges."

Longshot nodded. "Oh, yeah."

Together, Longshot and Kabed said, "You just have to hover." They laughed at their simultaneous response.

"Kabed, you're a man after my own heart," Longshot said merrily.

"Yes," Kabed agreed. "Perhaps we *should* go to the taverns some day and see who has the greater charms."

"Heck yeah! Of course, I wouldn't follow through on anything. Just see if I can *interest* more folks than you. I love my princess, and I'm chomping at the bit to get out of here and rescue her from that monster in Mech Valley."

Joryn patted Longshot on the shoulder. "The moment will come, my friend. I promise you. And, as for Starro," he smirked, shaking his head with amusement, "just don't worry about it."

"You know something, don't you? That guy has a secret! I can tell from your face. Tell me! He's so *proper.* I've gotta know! I can't even picture him with a lover. Even when I thought he was married, I pictured her all plain and shapeless and boring as a snowball fight in Hell to be *with* that guy."

Joryn laughed out loud. "Longshot, even if I did know a secret, I could hardly share it then, could I?"

"Well, sure. Not if you're *honorable.*" He waited.

And waited.

"Oh, right. You *are* honorable. Well, I'll figure it out. Just you wait."

Joryn only laughed, as he tried to think of his sister, Princess Willowyll, as anything even *remotely* plain or shapeless.

As Captain Starro made his way through the palace hallways to his destination, he was surprised by the voice of the crown prince.

"Starro! Can I have a moment?"

The captain stopped and turned. "Prince Kail. Of course. How may I be of service?"

"I come not as your prince, but as your friend in this matter. I've just come from council. I thought you should know …"

"Know what, my prince?"

Somberly, Kail proceeded, "My father plans to find a husband for Princess Willowyll. He's seeking suitors from powerful kingdoms, to strengthen alliances."

Though he said nothing, the color drained instantly from Starro's face.

"Willowyll doesn't know yet," Kail added.

"Forgive me, my prince, but what does it matter to me? I am only the captain of the Guard. I know nothing about arranging courtly suitors, if that's what you're asking of me."

"Starro, listen to me," Kail said solemnly. "I *know*."

The captain met Kail's eyes, listening, but revealing nothing.

"I am only warning you, because I would otherwise support you in this, if I could. You're a good man. A worthy man. But you know my father and the Council. Amazingly, no one else on the Council has figured it out, considering how obsessed they seem to be with the amorous adventures of my siblings, but as for me and my brothers and sisters, there is no doubt among any of us as to where you are headed even now. Not even Repteré is troubled by it. We all love you. You must know it."

"My prince …" Starro was nonplussed.

Kail nodded and patted the guardsman on the shoulder, understanding. "So, as I was saying, Starro … Warn her for me. I know you two aren't close at all, but you know what a coward I am. I could never tell her what Father intends for her myself."

The captain nodded. "You may count on me, my prince."

"Thank you, Starro. And please, do not report my cowardice to anyone. I'd hate to lose face."

"Certainly not, my prince. There is nothing of the sort to report."

Kail nodded, smiled. "I'm off to find Joryn. We have similar news to break to Prince Vail." He sighed, as he walked away, and groaned, only half-joking, "What has the Council of Advisors become?"

Joryn lay on his bed, back in his room, wondering whether he should call Galen again, or if it was too soon. This long-distance relationship was driving him insane. He sighed miserably.

A knock at his door took him from his thoughts. "Come in."

The door opened. "You're very trusting, Little Brother."

Joryn smiled. "You have a distinctive knock."

"If you say so," Kail said with a smile.

"So, what news do you bring from the Council meeting?"

"To be brief, your mission to Mech Valley and a week's holiday to the Whispering Plains thereafter have been approved. That's the bright side of it."

"And the other side?" Joryn asked, dreading the answer.

"The Council is overly concerned with the love interests of the royal offspring, and Father has agreed to start marrying off our sisters to strengthen alliances with kingdoms of wealth and power, beginning with the oldest."

"So they have broken Starro's heart as well as Willowyll's?"

"They know nothing of that tryst. But as for Vail …"

"Oh, poor Vail! He's gone into the Spiritwood Forest just this morning to see her! Are they going to find a powerful wife for him too?"

"Not yet, but Father has said the relationship must end."

Worried, Joryn asked, "Do you agree with him?"

"I don't know. I suppose I think it is pointless to tell someone that they cannot love the one they love. How can anyone stop it? He will always love her, and he will only resent being told that he must not see her again. I don't know what the right thing is here. But on the other hand, she *is* an immortal. Only tragedy can come of it."

"So I've heard, time and again," Joryn agreed solemnly. "Parakletos drove the point home one time, when he was teaching me all of the old myths. But still, I enjoy seeing Vail's heart so light. I would hope they became the exception to those old cautionary tales."

"I would hope so too," Kail said. "But they would have to do so in secret. Either way, they must be warned, and the decision must be left to them."

"Yes."

"So, are you up for a ride, before you gather your men and head for Mech Valley?"

"Are we off to Spiritwood Forest?"

"Where else?"

"Then of course. I won't leave you to carry out such a miserable task alone. I'll get Illium."

"Charger already has. They'll be waiting at the front gates."

"You know me well then." Joryn laughed, getting to his feet.

"Of course I do, Little Brother. I *raised* you well."

The two brothers left Joryn's room and made their way to the front gates of the palace and a mission together to deliver the bitter news to Prince Vail.

"Willowyll," Starro said brightly, as he walked into the palace garden.

"Starro! I thought you would never get here." She lit up at the sight of him and ran to him, kissing him on the lips without further preamble.

He pulled back, laughing. "My love, what of the guards?"

She winked. "You mean the ones you *never* assign to any place within sight of the garden on this hour of this day, every single week? Somehow, I'm not concerned we'll be discovered."

"Clever princess!" He held her in his arms, then led her by the hand to a bench by the little stream that passed through the flowers and trees. They sat down together, and he said, "But it seems the guards are not as clever as your eleven brothers and sisters."

"Oh?"

His face darkened.

"What is it, Starro?"

"Prince Kail stopped me in the hall, with a warning. Your father means to find a husband for you."

"What? That can't be! Father has *never* done such a thing. I always assumed it would be *my* choice when the time came to marry."

"The Council may have influenced him then, but Kail gave me the news to deliver to you. While I confessed nothing, he assured me that he knows everything, though the Council does not. He tells me *all* of your siblings know."

"I have told no one. Oh, those wretched children!" she giggled, but stopped abruptly, her face going serious. It was a transition she could make so startlingly fast, from playful to pragmatic, and Starro had never gotten used to it. "Then we must present you as my suitor. It is as simple as that. We have never discussed marriage, but if I must be courted openly, I choose you, and we can prolong the courtship for as long as you like. I will not force you to choose me for your wife."

He pulled her hand to his lips, kissed her knuckles. "If it were my choice to make, my Willowyll, I would court you for but a day, and the marriage would commence."

She gasped, her eyes tearing up.

"But, your father means for you to marry a nobleman."

"What?" She stood, outraged. "Who? Has he chosen someone already?"

Starro stood as well, trying to calm her. "Apparently not. But the purpose of your marriage will be to strengthen an alliance.

Your brother told me nothing more than this. Aside from the fact that all who know of our love approve of it. He wished he could support us."

"Well then, why doesn't he? Where is he now? I will demand his support!"

"And go public with our relationship?" Starro asked, gently. "Tell your father, *your* father, that you will not court for politics, but for love? Tell him that it is I who stands between you and a noble husband?"

"You're right," she said, her voice quieting with sorrow. "He would have your head. At the very least, you'd be driven from the palace, from the Empire of Nod altogether."

"But I will risk it, if it is what you want, Willowyll." He pulled her to him, kissed her again.

"We could run away together," she said, pulling back.

"Or we could fight here for our love *first*," Starro suggested. "Either way, the consequences to you are unbearable for me to consider. A princess with a broken heart, or a princess on the run. Neither will do."

"There is much to consider," she agreed, shaking her head with resignation. "For the future. But the present …"

He smiled, as he held her close. "The present is ours. We need not make a decision. Not right now."

"No," she agreed with a tearful smile. "In the days ahead, we'll decide what to do, but the decision for *this* moment is perfectly clear." She caressed his cheek, gazed into his deep, gray eyes.

Without another word, they kissed again, allowing the moment to linger this time, leaving the burdens of the future to their own time, with none to witness their love save for the flowers that surrounded them.

Chapter 5:
The Clocks Strike

THROUGHOUT THE EMPIRE OF NOD, IT WAS COURTSDAY, the one day of the month when the emperor held court and allowed the people to bring their grievances and gifts to him in person, one at a time. In the spirit of Courtsday, the other kings and governors throughout the Empire honored the tradition in their own provinces, and few audience chambers were as magnificent to behold as that of the sparklingly bejeweled tower of Lord Pleidies, in the Whispering Plains.

Galen and his cousin Everron were present, standing to the side of the glistening Seat of Governance where Galen's father sat. Several of the Plains people had been escorted in and back out again already, and Everron was beginning to tire.

"Is it always this tedious?" Everron asked his cousin in a conspiratorial whisper.

"Not always. Some months it gets rather exciting. The people aren't always so pleasant. So far, none have come with a grievance."

"What does my uncle do with all of these gifts?" Everron asked.

Galen shrugged, a laugh in his voice, "I honestly have no idea."

The guards announced the next visitor to the governor. "We present Brother Clock, of Mountain Town."

A man in a hooded cloak strode into the room and kneeled before the Seat of Governance.

"Please rise, Brother Clock," said Lord Pleidies pleasantly. "Mountain Town? I've not heard of that. Surely it's not within our province?"

"No, my lord, it is not," the man said in a raspy voice that echoed strangely within his robes.

Everron gestured with a nod towards the table and whispered to Galen, "I'm going to refill my goblet."

"Oh, no," Galen insisted. "I'll do it for you." He snatched the goblet from his cousin's hand with a grin and reveled in the excuse to step away from the throne for a moment. "Be right back, Cousin."

"Bastard," Everron whispered facetiously, suppressing his own laughter.

***

At the very same moment, an identical visitor, also called Brother Clock, was announced at Palace Nod in the capital city, where the emperor was holding his own Courtsday audiences.

"I have never heard of Mountain Town," Sapros said, crossly. He noticed a ticking sound that seemed to be coming from the robed man. "Who are you? Where are you from? What do you want here?"

"You have not heard of Mountain Town," said Brother Clock, in his raspy, echoing voice, "because it does not exist as such. It has long been known to all, however, as Mount Dread."

"Mount—? Is this a joke?" The emperor was furious. "Guards!"

Brother Clock removed his hood then, revealing a head and chest that were entirely mechanical, filled with moving gears, and fashioned out of wood. "I bring a gift from the Wanderer of legend."

"Madness!" the emperor shouted, as he stood from his throne.

The guards approached Brother Clock, taking him by the arms.

Brother Clock was unmoved, as he added, "The gift of your death, to the people of Nod."

The ticking grew louder, coming from the man himself, and the emperor realized all too late what the ticking foretold. "Get down! Everyone—!"

Before Emperor Sapros could finish his command, Brother Clock exploded.

As Galen made his way across the room to the table, his father asked the stranger, "How may the Lord of Pleidies Tower be of service to you then, good traveler?"

The echoing, raspy voice spoke again from beneath the great hood, "You may accept this gift, from the Wanderer of legend."

"From the who? What are you talking about—?"

"And then," Brother Clock said, removing his hood, "you may die, false governor of the Empire of Lies."

Lord Pleidies rose, horrified at the sight of the ticking, clockwork man before him. "How dare you!"

Galen realized what was happening, looked to the blissfully amused face of his cousin standing by the throne unaware of any danger, then to the outraged face of his father, who also failed to suspect the true nature of Brother Clock. He dropped his cousin's full goblet to the ground without hesitation and, out of sheer habit, he reached for the pistol at his side and drew it, though he knew it would do no good. "Father! Move! Everyone get out!" He took one step to run towards his father from across the room, only to be blown off of his feet and sent flying violently backwards by the terrible force and scalding wind of the explosion that brought his father's audience chamber, in all of its glistening beauty, collapsing down on top of them.

***

It was a moment of horror that unfolded similarly in every province of Nod, in the court of every king, governor, and ally of the Empire. In all but the city of Din, the devastation brought by the Brothers Clock was more than anyone had been prepared for. Before the dust of the first explosion had settled, the death toll throughout the land had already reached numbers beyond counting.

CHAPTER 6:
AFTERSHOCK

UNAWARE OF THE CRISIS UNFOLDING ACROSS THE EMpire, Kail and Joryn had ridden quickly on the backs of their unicorn steeds from the palace, through the city streets, and all the way to the outskirts of the royal city, where they met their brother Vail, who was humming a silly song astride the Unitron he had once again stolen from Kabed's den of technological wonders.

"And who is this starry-eyed fool I see before me?" Kail shouted in loving jest.

Vail slowly took notice of the fact that he was observed and laughed like just the absent-minded fool his latest love affair had made of him. "Hello, noble brothers. Have you come to wreck my mood?" He rode over to them, as they waited.

When Vail brought the Unitron to a stop just in front of Kail and Joryn, Kail nodded sadly, hating to become the enemy of his brother's newfound bliss. "Perhaps. We should talk. Are you up for a ride?"

Vail shrugged. "Sounds fantastic, if you think that Charger and Illium can keep up with …" he regarded his robotic steed, "… Unitron 003."

He patted the synthetic unicorn on the shoulder. "You know, Unitron 003, we're going to have to come up with a proper name for you, if I'm going to keep stealing you. How about Lance? I mean, you've got one attached to your head, so we might as well take the name before someone else does, right?" He awaited the robot's response for only an instant, before declaring with autocratic delight, "It's settled then, Unitron 003; you are henceforth Lance."

"Command acknowledged," the newly named Lance said in its computerized voice. "New designation: Lance, by your command, Prince Vail."

Vail giggled. "I love this guy. Unitrons are awesome. Where shall we ride to?"

"Anywhere, if it keeps us from watching you make love to your steed," Joryn teased. "And here I thought you had come to meet Merridy again."

Guiding Lance, Vail fell into step beside his brothers, and they turned to head back towards the palace together. "Ah, Merridy, my soul's own melody! I love her, Joryn. I am certain I am in love. I am most sincere. She's the very answer to my heart's call."

Joryn looked to Kail.

Kail cleared his throat, reluctantly. "About that, Vail. Father has—"

"What's that?" Vail cut him off, urgently, staring into the distance.

The other two princes and their steeds followed Vail's gaze, and their eyes widened in horror.

"By all the gods. It's Courtsday," Kail said, a terrified tremor in his voice.

"We thought it was thunder!" Joryn realized, wracked with dread and remorse. "Illium, to the palace, as fast as your legs will carry us!"

Illium complied, wordlessly, urgently, and Charger and Lance raced to keep up, carrying the princes towards the palace, and the ominous cloud of smoke rising from the eastern side, where they all knew the throne room to be located, and all the way up to the sky.

Drae Shivvan made his way through the corridor towards Quickwing's quarters, his reasons for the visit having been forgotten at the moment of the explosion. At the rumbling of the walls and the floor beneath his feet, the warrior part of the Highland Elf had taken over, and he made his way to the Celestian's room now only to have an ally in facing whatever sinister force had caused the sound and tremor that had surely been the result of a bomb. He heard a commotion, as he neared Quickwing's door, and wondered if the enemy had already found the winged warrior.

The door flying from its hinges and into the wall across the hall soon answered his question.

Quickwing stepped out into the hallway, his senses clearly on alert. He noticed the elf. "Shivvan! What has happened?"

"I don't know. Are you all right?" He indicated the broken door with a worried glance.

"Yes," Quickwing assured him. "The tremor had jammed the door. The entire palace must have shifted." He flexed his wings, winced in pain. "You have to get to the throne room, Shivvan. It's Courtsday. The emperor must be protected, and the enemies of Palace Nod must be brought to justice."

"You speak as if you'll not be joining me," the elf observed.

"What use would I be? I am lame. I would only get in your way."

"In case you hadn't noticed, Quickwing, I am not in the best of shape myself these days. I have a chronic pain since Chiroptera. The pills the priestess of Libran has given me are all that keep me moving. I have only a small window of usefulness before the pain overtakes me again. I cannot go seeking the source of this explosion alone. It may be nothing. An accident with one of those new flying discs, an explosion of some experiment-gone-wrong in Kabed's workshop. But it could be something more malicious. It could be the Chiropterans, turning their back on the treaty. We *must* find out the truth. *Both* of us."

"But my wings …"

"Wouldn't do for stealth in this instance anyway. I need your help, Quickwing. Really, I'm only offering you mine. I will fall from my injury much sooner than you from yours. My pills are back in my quarters, and we dare not take the time now to go back for them. Believe me; *you* are the worthier hero here. Now, let's stop feeling sorry for ourselves and see to this explosion." Drae moved past the Celestian, down the hallway.

Reluctantly, Quickwing nodded his head and followed.

In the communications center, the palace operator, Golan Binju, struggled to get the com screen system back online in order to call for help. When at last the monitor came to life and began picking up a signal, however, he found it flooded with messages and incoming calls from across the Empire. Every single principality had been hit by whatever terrorist regime had struck the Imperial palace, it seemed; at least, every one that had opted to adopt the com screen communications network. Every time that Golan tried to make a call out, he was stopped by a flashing light that indicated an incoming call, and he sent the call to be recorded and dealt with later. Finally, he realized that the only way he was likely to get word *out* about the palace's situation was to take a call that was coming *in*. As expected, another flashing light indicated an incoming call. He opened the channel. "Palace Nod, this is Golan, how may I—?"

"Is *this* our reward for allying ourselves with the Empire?" The young Chirop's face was covered in blood, matting the fur of his cheeks. Behind him, wires dangled, smoke framed his image, and it was clear the mountain stronghold of the proud race of bat people had sustained tremendous damage.

"I'm just now getting the palace back online," Golan explained. "I suspect whoever hit your mountain also hit the Imperial palace and every other principality of the Empire. Who may I say is—?"

"This was, until moments ago, Prince Orlok the Younger. Now, I am *King* Orlok II. My father is dead. Taken to the grave by a suicide bomber. Some sort of clockwork humanoid who claimed to serve the Wanderer and held us in contempt for our alliance with the Empire. What is *Emperor* Sapros planning to do about it, Operator?" The new king spat the words, presently furious and disgusted with the entire human race.

With deep compassion, Golan lowered his head. "Your Majesty, the entire empire is wounded by your loss. I must also confess I do not know that the palace has fared any better than Chiroptera. The fate of the emperor is unknown. The palace is in chaos. Please, help spread the word. If we can send aid, we will. Please make contact with as many of our allies as you can. The whole empire is in crisis."

"Forgive me," Orlok said. "I saw only my own catastrophe. Our hearts are with you. I will try to make contact with the other monarchs and governors, to the best of my ability. Our own operator is injured and unconscious at present. But I will do what I can. Stay strong, Golan. Death before surrender!" The newly named king of Chiroptera ended the transmission.

Golan took the next call, hoping to find someone who could send aid at the other end. He took in the sight of the young human on the screen, covered in dirt and blood, his clothes torn to rags. "Lord Galen!"

"Golan, we've been attacked!"

"I know. We were hit as well. It seems this happened all over the Empire. I've only just restored communications here. The Chirops have lost their king and gained another. I have no idea the status of the emperor. How is your father?"

"He's …" Galen struggled to hold back tears of fear and rage. "He's in the med center. They don't know if he'll ever wake up. The bomb, the *living* bomb, went off in the main audience chamber. Many were injured. Some were killed. I've taken charge until my father regains consciousness. Is there any help you can send us? The tower was almost destroyed."

"I will let you know as soon as possible, my lord. I'm afraid we're still taking in the damage here. I was hoping to find help myself. Please help spread the word. Every ruler of every principality will have to send or receive aid as they can, all across the Empire."

Galen nodded, and he tried to say more, but the screen went to static at his end, and the channel was lost.

Golan at last had an opening, and he made a call out. The dragons of Din had recently agreed to join the com screen network, just as they had recently become the Empire's most powerful allies.

The dragon operator answered, and Golan was in awe of the sight of her, having never seen a dragon with his own eyes before. "This is the Palace of Din. Why do you trouble us?"

"I mean no trouble. This is Operator Golan Binju, at Palace Nod. We've been attacked by unknown enemies, as has the whole of our empire. We were hoping to enlist your aid."

The dragon glared at the human operator, smoke rolling gently out of her elongated mouth as she huffed. "Our queen has already spoken on this matter. You speak of these mechanical bomber men, do you not?"

"Yes! Were you hit as well?"

"So to speak, but it was of no consequence. Queen Shaakkanaah stomped on the fool the moment he openly wished her dead. He exploded beneath her mighty foot. It was a pathetic display."

"I'm afraid the rest of our allies were not so fortunate," Golan told her. "Would you be willing to send aid to the Empire in this matter?"

"The queen does not think so. She has declared this a *human* matter; an internal affair to be dealt with by humans alone. She has no love for this *Wanderer*. He has caused the land much grief over the millennia."

"But surely he can't actually be *the* Wanderer. The Wanderer was killed by Palo centuries ago, if he even existed. He's a legend. Invoking his name is likely nothing more than a terrorist fear tactic."

"Oh," the dragon operator assured Golan smugly, "I am sure you are mistaken. The Wanderer is very real, and this is just the sort of thing that he would do. He had been around for almost three-thousand years *before* Bran, before Palo, and we dragons know all too well what use it is to *kill* such an abomination of nature as the Wanderer. We have despised him since he first appeared in Nod. There were *no* humans in Nod whatever before he was sent here, along with the so-called Twelve Great Gods that followed. We have no use for them. He brought all that is wrong with Nod, and he is a nuisance to us, but a bane to the humans. We are certain the Wanderer has returned, and the queen has, as I said, declared it a human problem. A worthy test of the one we revere among you; the champion of Libran."

"But—" Golan was unable to say anything more, before the dragon abruptly ended the transmission on her end.

A new, raspy, metallic voice caused Golan to turn around in his seat with surprise. "Naughty, naughty!" The robotic menace before him raised its arm, and a gun that seemed a part of the arm itself lifted out of the top of it and fired a light ray at the control panel, destroying it and ending any hope of further transmissions.

"Who … *What* are you?" Golan demanded, as he stood to face the intruder.

"I am called Jakknife," the thing said, as it retracted the gun and released several long, deadly blades from its torso, twirling them around in a show of dominance. "I'm basically every terrible weapon you could dream of, spliced into a living, sociopathic, if not decidedly *evil* machine. And you're coming with me, my little tattletale."

Golan studied the blades the being swiveled idly in his direction and swallowed audibly, as sweat began beading on his forehead. He'd done what he could. Now it was up to Orlok, Galen, and perhaps the dragons of Din, to spread the word of their plight. "It seems I have little choice in the matter."

"Smart for an organic, aren't you?" Jakknife retracted his blades and grabbed the human operator by the collar, carrying him from the communication center to whatever fate awaited him.

***

"Unhand me, diarrhea breath!" demanded the diminutive Onri Sprigg to the giant creature who carried him in one claw and a wounded Dorran Equus in the other.

"Pipe down, pipsqueak," the creature snapped. "Your ire is nothing against a demigod such as me."

"He's right, for now, Sprigg," Dorran grumbled. "We must bide our time."

The creature laughed. "Indeed? What time is that, centaur? We're only keeping you alive to face the Wanderer."

Dorran paled. "Surely you—"

"No, I'm as serious as a dismembered unicorn." The monster laughed, as though he'd told a joke that anyone at all should get.

As the creature entered the emperor's audience chamber, Kabed, seated on the floor with his hands and legs bound, comprehended his identity. "You're Warclaw! You're the one who nearly killed Illium!"

"The one and only." The enormous crab man tossed his prisoners to the ground.

The two heroes struggled to get to their feet, but ropes came at them, seemingly of their own volition, and tied themselves around their wrists and ankles.

"Nice trick, Gemino," Warclaw said, nodding to the young man, "Gemina," he nodded to the man's twin sister.

Gemino shrugged. "Parlor tricks really."

Gemina laughed. "Yes. We could do a lot more damage with our sorcery, if the Wanderer hadn't wanted the survivors *kept* survivors until he arrived."

"True," Gemino agreed. He nodded ahead. "*That* one was far more fun than playing with these ropes."

Warclaw followed the young sorcerer's nod to see a giant birdcage, apparently made of light, in which sat the helpless priestess of Libran and her Deluvian warbird. Warclaw laughed even harder. "This was easy! Some great heroes. I told you they were weak. At least their wimp leader and his should-be-dead unicorn. I don't know what all the hype is about. So he *talked* to some dragons, and he *stunned* some Chirops. Big deal. I ripped his unicorn's legs off and left them both for dead. Twice. Nothing they could do to *talk* me out of it neither."

"You won't get away with this," the priestess said. "You shouldn't be so boastful before *all* of our heroes are accounted for."

"We'll have them all soon enough, little priestess. The ones we haven't captured are surely dead anyway. Those Brother Clocks really pack a wallop."

"I think this does it," a new voice broke in.

"By the fires of the nine hells," Dorran grunted to Kabed, "what is *that*?"

"It's a fingrin," Kabed answered. "Shark people. Barbaric sea dwellers. Enemies of Deluvia. Don't let him kiss you."

"Oh, I'll keep that in mind." Dorran laughed nervously, studying the monster's numerous rows of metal teeth.

The fingrin laughed, as he led an army of robotic soldiers into the room, each carrying a prisoner. "We rounded up all of the royal whelps and their mothers."

Kabed studied the new arrivals, taking a mental inventory. Already present and captured were himself, Dorran Equus, Onri Sprigg, the priestess Tianna, and Iron Bill. Tied into the throne was the unconscious, perhaps mortally wounded form of Emperor Sapros. Several of the palace guards were also tied up in various corners of the great room by the magic of the twin sorcerers. Many more guards than that lay dead all around them, lost in the explosion. No sign of Captain Starro or his second-in-command Lieutenant Moon. No sign of Longshot, Lowgun, Trig, Quickwing, or Drae Shivvan.

As for the royal family, the robot troops had just brought in, battered and bruised from obvious resistance, all of Sapros' surviving wives: the ambitious Lady Makhaira, with a complexion of snow and a heart of ice; dark-skinned Lady Amina, known for her love of peace and resistance to political intrigue; the somewhat rough-and-tumble Lady Leita, her piercing green eyes ever shifting, looking for an opening to make a break for it and give these robot troops what for; and lastly, Lady Riko, dark haired, with deep brown eyes that ever showed her mind at work behind them, and politically savvy enough to negotiate her way out of anything, until today it seemed.

He took a count of the sons and daughters as well. Princess Hero, the undeniable daughter of adventurous Lady Leita, had more bruises on her face than all the rest. She had clearly put up quite a fight. No sign of her brother Vail. That worried him. The fine line between bravery and stupidity was much more likely to be crossed by Vail than by his elder sister. If he had been killed … But hadn't he gone out riding this morning? The brat *had* stolen Unitron 003 again. Kabed held out hope that Vail had avoided the attack on the palace altogether.

And there were the offspring of Lady Makhaira. Her son, Sapros' second-born, ever-cunning and ambitious Prince Repteré, and his younger sister, the beautiful Princess Willowyll, oldest of Sapros' daughters and as wise in matters of courtly life and diplomacy as Prince Kail and Lady Riko.

The offspring of Lady Amina were likewise accounted for. Faithful, trusting Prince Dakarai, his bookish academic brother Prince Mwana, and their flighty but lovely sister Princess Adaeze, probably more upset that her expensively bejeweled gown had been torn than that anyone had been injured or killed.

Lady Riko's three were there as well, in the arms of the menacing ape-like robots. Prince Dorago, generally not one to draw attention to himself or to say more words than needed saying, but strong and brave enough to have almost as many bruises as Princess Hero; Princess Enjinia, likely already dirty from helping Kabed out in the workshop earlier that day. It was difficult to tell the bruises from the grease stains. And then there was Sapros' youngest daughter, the mysterious, almost frighteningly calm Princess Lily.

As for the sons of the late anointed queen, Kail and Joryn, Sapros' eldest and youngest respectively, were not among the prisoners. Kabed hoped upon hope that they, and Vail alike, were not in the palace at all, for Illium and Charger were likewise nowhere to be seen. Of course, the unicorns may have been anywhere when the attack had occurred.

Last of all, Kabed noted the presence of Prince Kail's wife, Princess Maressah, her long, curly blonde hair mussed, her clothes torn, but her countenance showing nothing of fear or weakness to her enemies. What a queen she would make after the time of Sapros, though such thoughts were forbidden by law.

The fingrin's teeth rotated in his mouth, not at all a natural trait for the species. This one's jaws had clearly been altered. "Razorwing was rounding up the last of the Imperial Guard," he said. He snapped his jaws loudly, and Kabed jumped where he sat, having seen fingrins up close in his youth and all of the terrors their massive jaws could inflict.

To Kabed's surprise, Princess Lily, who was standing closest to the monster, laughed as though the fingrin were the most pitiable of villains.

"Good," Warclaw said. "The Wanderer will be pleased."

"How so?" Gemina asked. "The emperor still lives, and Prince Joryn is not among the prisoners *or* the dead."

"I already told you, girl" Warclaw said agitatedly, "he's a weakling. A coward. His legend is nothing but just that. If he can't *talk* us to death, he's powerless. He may have been able to negotiate his way through with the dragons and the Chirops, but not my claws. And I assure you, the Wanderer does *not* negotiate."

A Chirop flew into the ruined audience chamber then, his wings having been surgically altered to attach the blades that had given him his name. There was something familiar about him, though Kabed could not quite place it. He had seen so many Chirops in the recent battle, but this one stood out somehow.

The Chirop, Razorwing, landed, and he was followed by two of the hulking robots, who held in their arms Captain Starro and Lieutenant Moon. "The guards have been subdued," he said.

The fingrin clashed his metal teeth together again, a show of aggression common to the warriors of his species. "Great! So now we wait. Why does the Wanderer want them alive anyway? It doesn't make any sense. First he bombs the palace, then he wants the survivors left alive."

The sorcerer Gemino laughed. "He's funny like that, I guess, Dreadfin. He's powerful enough that I don't question his somewhat manic agendas."

"Good point. At least we've done our job though."

"Hm," Razorwing considered. "I won't be comfortable with that statement until we've accounted for the rest of Prince Joryn's formidable entourage. By my count, we are still short the Celestian, the Highland Elf, the reptisaur, and—"

"Trig, switch!" Longshot shouted, as he burst into the room in a blaze of self-perceived heroic glory.

The mechanical horse leapt into the air and converted itself into a giant gun, fastening itself to the young human's arm and back.

Longshot boasted, his swagger undaunted by the sheer numbers he was going up against, "Don't worry; I'll save you, Princess Hero!"

The battered princess rolled her eyes. "Oh, will you give it up, trigger brain? And I'm not the only prisoner here!"

Ignoring the princess, Longshot and Trig opened fire, several of the ape-like robots taking the blast and falling before them.

From the ceiling, the reptilian hero Lowgun Kin dropped down silently, slashing through two robots with his swords, before Gemina and Gemino tripped him up with their magical ropes.

"Don't worry, buddy! I'll avenge you!" Longshot took aim at Warclaw, who managed to dodge the blast deftly, in spite of his bulk.

"Careful," Razorwing commanded. "This one gave us quite a test at Mount Chirop!"

So, Kabed noted to himself, *he* was *at the battle of Chiroptera.*

"Leave him to me!" Jakknife dropped Golan next to Kabed, as he entered the chamber, and he marched straight towards the youth and his shape-shifting horse gun.

"Oh, you want some of this, bolts-for-brains? Come on then! Yee-haw!"

Longshot fired Trig directly at the robotic warrior, but things did not go according to plan.

Jakknife's thick, round back plate swiveled up and over his head, glowing green with an energy field, and shielding him from Trig's blast, absorbing the energy.

As Longshot stood momentarily stunned, the robotic menace returned the shield to its place on his back, unsheathed a mace from the underside of his left arm, and knocked the young gunslinger and his weaponized steed aside like a pair of weeds.

The sorcerous twins quickly sent their ropes into action, tying Longshot's arms and legs and binding Trig so that he was trapped in his gun form, turning him on the ground and aiming him at Longshot, lest the transformed horse should decide to open fire.

"Had enough yet?" Longshot crowed defiantly from the floor, where he lay bound.

Dreadfin looked to Warclaw. "So, not only is Prince Joryn a weakling and a coward, but his elite are clearly idiots as well." The villains both laughed.

"Silence," Razorwing barked, holding Golan's com helmet in his hands. "This operator's helmet has up-to-date information on the status of all of the palace's inhabitants. The Celestian and the Highland Elf are both wounded, it seems. They will not be able to put up a fight once we find them. As for the three missing princes, they had all left the palace before our attack. Our troops in the city will easily keep them from returning here. Our task is accomplished. The time has come. Jakknife, open a channel to the *Darkstar*."

The robotic warrior stood before Razorwing and transmitted an image of the Chirop to their master aboard his flying command ship.

"Master," Razorwing said, "Palace Nod has fallen. The Empire of Nod is yours."

CHAPTER 7:
THE WANDERER RETURNS

THE GIANT AIR SHIP, THE *DARKSTAR*, DESIGNED TO resemble the long-fanged skull of a deadly snake, cast an ominous shadow over the still smoking Imperial palace, as it approached and then landed in the back, where all of the Fighter Discs had been parked in an open landing field.

A door on the side of the craft unsealed and slowly lowered, becoming a ramp, and a figure in a somewhat threadbare robe, with a horned mask over his face that was the impetus of many a would-be hero's nightmares, strode down, a green staff in his hand, forged in the likeness of a three-headed viper.

Razorwing and a contingent of the ape-like robot soldiers greeted the new arrival. "It is done, my master. The throne awaits you."

"You are to be commended, Razorwing," the very voice of evil echoed out of the mask. "It is a new dawn for humanity. A new day for Nod." The being known as the Wanderer strode ahead, as though he knew the layout of the palace well.

Razorwing struggled to keep up with his master's long strides. "The heroes of the palace have been rounded up and taken to the dungeon, along with the royal wives and potential successors. The emperor himself has just returned to consciousness tied in his throne, awaiting your judgment."

"Good! Very good!" The Wanderer cackled, and there was nothing but derision in the sound of his laughter.

As he entered the ruined throne room, the Wanderer paused to take in the damage. "Yes. This moment has been a long time in coming. For untold centuries, I've been planning my revenge, and now it is done." He surveyed the smoke and dust, the fallen stones, the bodies of the dead all around him. "Chaos is the very essence of beauty throughout the universe, and I am its creator. I am its very god."

He turned to the throne. "Pretender Sapros, I presume."

The wounded man on the throne, dried blood caked in his beard, one eye swollen shut, black and blue, spat blood at the floor before the Wanderer. "Who the hell are you, and what do you want here, so that I may deny you without a care?"

The Wanderer laughed, and a chill ran through all in the room at the sound, even his followers, whose fear of him far outweighed their loyalty. "Quite simple, young Sapros. I want this so-called empire that my progeny have built. I want to give myself to Nod once more. I am murder, I am guilt, I am hunger, I am revenge twice over, from the first days of humans in Nod, to the time of Bran and his foolish son, to the time of Palo, and until now, I am the master of the human race in this world, and I wish to share my very essence with all of my wayward children. Will you deny me that, false ruler? You have neither the authority nor the constitution, and your mighty defenders have already fallen to my own warriors. You are *emperor* no more."

A sound of movement and a light coughing caught the Wanderer's ears, and he turned to see a broken and bleeding guardsman who had been earlier dismissed as dead, looking up from the rubble and raising a light pistol in his direction.

Blood sputtered from the young man's mouth, as he coughed and managed the three words that were most important to him in his duty as a guardsman, "For … the … emperor!" He pulled the trigger.

The Wanderer sprang to action, spinning his staff around like a fan blade before him with supernatural speed, deflecting the initial blast and the two that followed. He strode over to the guardsman in a fury and kicked the gun from his hand without hesitation.

"You'll … never take … the palace …," the guardsman spat.

"Such foolish loyalty. Such misguided optimism." The Wanderer applied a booted foot to the guard's head, forcing it back down to the ground, where he began slowly applying pressure. The nauseous sound of the man's skull beginning to crack beneath the Wanderer's heal filled the room with horror, until, at last, the guard's head was crushed completely, and the Wanderer's boot hit the stone floor beneath it with a definitive thud. He turned to see the once proud Emperor Sapros shedding silent tears. Of sorrow? Of rage? It mattered not to the dark, heartless visage of the Wanderer. Though none could see his face behind the terrible mask he wore, he smiled hatefully. "Take the pretender to the dungeon with his wives and children."

"But," Gemino protested, "don't you want to kill him?"

The Wanderer turned on the young sorcerer with such fury that Gemino felt himself grow faint. "Did I not speak *clearly* enough for you, Gemino? I said to take him to the dungeon!"

"Y-y-yes, Master." Gemino bowed, and with his sister approached the throne and lifted the weakened Sapros.

The Wanderer turned to Jakknife. "Have you established a link with the com screen network?"

"Yes, Master."

"And hacked through into the holographic projectors in all of the town centers?"

"Of course."

"Good. I want all of the citizens of this so-called empire to know that they have been conquered." The Wanderer walked to the throne and took his place as the new ruler. "Transmit this, immediately."

Joryn, Kail, and Vail neared the road to the palace in the capital city, but were blocked, as a swarm of robots flew down from the sky and commanded in voices similar to, yet noticeably deeper than, those of the Unitrons, "Surrender to the Wanderer, humans."

"What are these?" Joryn asked.

Vail assessed the new arrivals. "Those, my brother, appear to be robot gorillas, with jetpacks and laser rifles."

"Of course," Kail said. "What else would they be?"

Trying and failing to tally the robots who continued to land, Joryn drew his sword and ordered calmly, "Fall back. We'll have to find another way to the palace."

The robot soldiers opened fire with their rifles, and the three brothers were able to dodge any shots that they did not block with their shields, as they made their way on their steeds back into the city.

At the city center, an image suddenly appeared over the great fountain, transmitted through the com screen network. Joryn gasped. "Again, I ask, what is *that*?"

"People of the upstart *Empire* of Nod!" The monstrous image said. "Your government has fallen. I am the Wanderer of your ancient legends. I am murder and remorse. I am hunger and vengeance upon vengeance. I am the progenitor of your race, and I am your rightful god! I have taken the throne of the Empire. The false emperor and all of his sons and daughters will be executed, publicly, at sunrise. Henceforth, any who rise up against me, any who dare to *speak* against my reign, will be summarily executed. I am your god; I am the Wanderer of your stories and myths, and I have spoken!" The transmission ended abruptly, replaced once again by the shimmering fountain.

"It can't be," Vail said.

"Father?" Charger asked the older unicorn.

Illium nodded. "My friends, we are in trouble."

The robot gorillas began making their way into the city square. "Bow down to the Wanderer," they demanded. "Bow down to the god of murder and despair. Bow down to the emperor of revenge."

A man approached the three princes, speaking for a large group of onlookers. "I know who you are, and we will not submit so long as you remain free. We will stand with you."

Kail nodded to the man. "Tell your people we are humbled by your loyalty. We will not abandon you, though I am unsure how we will prevail. There will be no consequences for those who choose to submit to these numbers before we find a way to defeat them."

The man nodded back and immediately began conspiring with his friends.

Joryn clearly heard the man say, "The champion of Libran is here. We have nothing to fear. Prepare to make a stand. Tell everyone to get ready for a fight. We have nothing to fear."

Feeling sick, Joryn said to his brothers, "How am I to stand with these townspeople *and* save the palace? My exaggerated reputation is suffocating us. I can't do it all. I'm not a god. These people have misplaced their faith."

"You are right, Little Brother," Kail said. "You cannot be everywhere at once. But you *are* here. Right now. And you are not alone. Remember that the palace is *full* of heroes these days. We must trust in *them* to do what can be done where they find themselves. We can only deal with one crisis at a time, and fate has placed us here."

"Yes," Joryn agreed. "You are right, as always, Kail. We must stand with the people of Nod. Here and now." He turned to Vail. "How familiar are you with Lance's systems?"

Vail shrugged. "Fairly familiar."

"I heard Kabed once say the Unitrons could tap into communication frequencies via an audio signal. Do you know anything about that?"

"No," Vail confessed, "But I bet Lance does. What do you say, Lance? Can you tap into the com network?"

"Affirmative," Lance said in his electronic voice.

"Good," Joryn said. "Try to get in touch with *any* of our friends at the palace. Try to find out what's going on."

"Command acknowledged," the Unitron said. "Attempting to locate an open channel."

A barrage of laser fire hit the statue at the heart of the great fountain then and brought it crumbling down.

"Submit or be executed." The lead robot commanded the crowd. "You have been ordered. Why do you not bow down?"

The robots surveyed the growing mob, assessing the situation and calling upon their programming to determine how to proceed.

The man who had spoken to the princes shouted out in defiance. "We will not submit! We stand with Prince Joryn, the Peace-Bringer! We do not fear you!"

The lead robot followed the man's body language and honed in on Joryn. "Prince Joryn: identified. Prince Kail: identified. Prince Vail: identified. Sir Illium: identified." The robot turned back to the man who had spoken up, and it fired without further preamble straight into the man's chest, killing him instantly.

"No!!!" Joryn shouted out in horror.

"Execute Prince Joryn. Priority one."

The other robots joined in the chant. "Execute! Execute!" Laser fire poured into the crowd.

"Fall back!" Joryn shouted. "Everyone fall back!" He pointed with his sword, guiding the mob to retreat behind the buildings rather than stay exposed in the town square. "*Fall back*!"

Seated in the throne, the Wanderer turned to Razorwing. "Bring me the Sword of Libran. Long have I coveted the power of the hated ebony blade. Long have I awaited the time when I would corrupt its symbolism with the blood of my enemies."

Nervously, Razorwing replied, "Master, forgive me, but we do not have the Sword of Libran in our hands ... just yet."

The Wanderer regarded the Chirop warrior coldly. "What?"

"It seems that Prince Joryn and two of his brothers were not in the palace at the time of our attack. But we can rest assured they are unable to return to cause you any trouble."

The Wanderer stood, outraged. "Fool! When Bran held the Sword of Libran, there was *nothing* that could stop him, short of unleashing the Darkening Scourge which finally took his life! But even that ... That cost me so *much*! That is why this *Prince Joryn* was the *one* person I told you to be *certain* was dead before we arrived here! I should kill you where you stand, *Nightstorm*!"

The Chirop bowed his head, assuming that the use of his former name was an indication that he was no longer a commander in the forces of the Wanderer, and he prepared to be put to death.

But his master soon told him otherwise. "However, I still have use of your particular talents. Rest assured that I will punish you *severely* when the time is available. For now, I want Joryn dead, and I want that sword!" As an afterthought, he asked, "Which of his two brothers are with him?"

Even knowing what wrath would follow, Razorwing answered dutifully, "Prince Vail … and Prince Kail, Master."

"Prince *Kail*! The very heir to the throne! How *enormously* you have failed me, Razorwing! *Where are they*?"

"We have not yet found them, Master. We know only that they were not in the palace when the Brother Clock struck."

"I want them found! I want Kail and the other prince brought to me, to be executed with their family! And I want Joryn, the sword-bearer, killed on sight, the Sword and Shield of Libran brought directly here when this is done. I may not know where the heroes of old hid the Darkening Scourge away after Bran's fall, but my robot apes should be more than a match for this *new* hero."

One of the robotic apes spoke up then, as if on cue, "Master, a report from the city has just been transmitted. Prince Joryn and his brothers are leading a mob of rebels against our forces in the town square."

Razorwing perked up. "I will go at once, my master. We will—"

"No!" the Wanderer cut him off. "You have failed me more than enough for one day, Razorwing." He looked to the enormous crab-like demigod. "Warclaw, you have defeated this upstart hero and his steed more than once."

Warclaw nodded. "With great pleasure, Master."

"It is unlikely that Libran will directly intervene, having by now equipped his new champion with enough allies to balance our threat. Take your own squadron of Gor'borgs into the city. Find Joryn and his brothers and carry out my will."

"I look forward to finishing the job this time," Warclaw pronounced.

"Then go!" the Wanderer raged. "Waste no more time! And do not return until it is done!"

Warclaw bowed his head, then turned, summoning a group of robotic apes to follow him, and confidently strode out of the decimated audience chamber.

CHAPTER 8:
THE BATTLE FOR IMPERIAL CITY

"EXECUTE!"

Laser fire knocked down a portion of the wall right beside Joryn's head.

"Execute the twelfth-born prince!"

More laser fire from the oncoming robot horde.

"Fall back!" Joryn said yet again, and the people obeyed. To Kail and Vail, he said, "Why do they keep *repeating* their orders out loud like that?"

"Haven't you figured it out?" Kail asked, as he raised his shield to deflect more laser blasts. "It's because they're stupid."

"Which probably means they're not sentient," Vail said. "Unlike Iron Bill and Trig, they're not *living* things."

"If only we could be sure," Joryn sighed.

The synthetic voice of Lance chimed in, "Scan of the enemy reveals limited brain function. Limited capacity for innovation. Designed for receiving and carrying out orders relevant to their pre-programmed skills. Sentience level: zero."

"See?" Kail said. "Stupid."

"Good," Joryn said, "so we can 'kill' them. We just need to figure out how."

More laser fire as the hulking robots slowly meandered around the corner. "Execute Joryn of Nod! Execute the pretender prince!"

"Fall back!"

"You can't just keep falling back," Kail said. "We're going to run out of buildings."

"I know that!" Joryn snapped, irritably. "I'm thinking!"

"Is your shield magic?" Vail asked.

"What?" Joryn studied Vail's face and saw that he indeed found the question relevant. "The Sword and Shield are only symbols."

"Is it a *magic* symbol?"

"I don't know."

"I bet it's a magic symbol." Without another interrogative or explanatory word, Vail snatched the shield from his youngest brother and threw it like a sportsdisc into the face of the nearest of the robot soldiers.

The shield spun through the air, tearing through the metal soldier's head like melted butter, leaving a sparking mess behind and circling on to the next of the deadly mechanicals.

A full line of troops stopped in their tracks, their heads engulfed in flame and smoke, and fell forward, deactivated.

The shield circled back and returned to Vail's hands. Delighted, he handed it back over to his brother. "Magic."

"Execute the enemy of the Wanderer!"

Joryn raised the magical ebony-hued shield and blocked three laser bolts that would have hit him directly in the head. "Magic shield. Stupid robots. Right, so, here's the plan." Joryn handed the shield back to Vail and rode Illium directly towards the oncoming troops.

"What in the hell is he doing?" Kail asked.

"I don't know, but I approve." Vail laughed. "My kind of plan."

"But his shield!"

The brothers watched as Joryn blocked another laser blast with his sword.

"Magic sword," said Vail. "And I think I get it."

Illium, shifting from stun to a more powerful light ray setting, fired back into the unliving soldiers with the guns at his sides, forcing the rest of the sinister robots to stop and process what had happened.

"What are you waiting for?" Joryn shouted to the robots, as he and Illium rode past. "I am Joryn of Nod! Execute!"

This declaration snapped the robots out of their brief reverie. "Execute Joryn of Nod!" They turned and began to follow him, leaving the people at their backs.

"Execute!"

"Execute the twelfth-born pretender child of Sapros!"

"See?" Vail said. "Brilliant!" He threw the Shield of Libran again, and it took down another row of robots from behind before returning to his hands.

"Attack!" Kail shouted to the waiting mob of citizens.

The mob rushed forward, with swords, battleaxes, daggers, and whatever other weapons they had grabbed when the trouble had begun, and proceeded to chop and stab through the armor plating of the robots' backs.

After a time, Joryn and Illium circled back around and rejoined Kail and Vail and the other two steeds. "I'm so glad that worked." Joryn caught his breath. "Stupid, right? They can't multi-task. It's either force the townspeople into submission or execute me. Clearly one is listed as a higher priority in their data banks."

"Do you want your shield back, Brother? Ever? Because I would gladly keep it for you," Vail asked, teasingly.

Joryn held out his hand to take back the shield with a smile. "I need to try this out myself." He rode ahead and threw the shield as Vail had done, watching it tear through the backs of the robots as it spun majestically through the air. When the shield returned to his hands, he laughed out loud. "Magic it is. Good call, Vail."

"That's the only kind I make."

"I'd better ride around again, so that the robots don't shift priorities and turn on the people."

"Channel opened," Lance announced suddenly.

"What?" Joryn asked. "What do you mean?"

"Joryn, is that you?" It was the voice of Quickwing coming through the Unitron's speakers.

"Lance! You're a wonder! Quickwing, yes, it's me. I'm in the city. What's your status?"

"Drae and I are in the air vents. The palace has fallen to a bunch of terrorist monsters with robotic apes of some sort. We've never seen anything like them."

"We've met the apes. We're fighting some of them now. What of our warriors? My brothers and sisters? And the emperor?"

"Rounded up. Many of the guards are dead. Your father and all of the rest of our friends have been taken to the dungeon. We're just gathering intel. Spying. Trying to determine a plan for action."

"Keep it up, Miiko. We've found the robots' critical weakness here. They can't multi-task. They're not bright at all. In fact, they're really, *really* stupid. Not even remotely sentient. We'll get to you as soon as we can."

"That's good," Quickwing said with relief, "because there's really nothing that I can do *but* spy in my condition."

A shadow fell over Joryn then, a familiar shadow that inspired his deepest fears to resurface—the shadow of one who had hurt him terribly in battle more than once. "Quickwing, I'm gonna have to call you back."

"New orders!" the source of the shadow commanded the robot apes. "Burn the city! Burn all of the buildings! Execute any who get in your way."

The new influx of soldiers he had brought with him joined in with the others who still remained. "Burn the city!" they parroted.

"Execute any who get in the way!" The robots turned, and several opened fire into the crowd, striking down a number of the rebellious townspeople.

Joryn watched on in stunned horror.

"Joryn! Come back to us! What is it?" Kail asked.

"That's him. That's the monster who almost killed Illium. The demigod who left us for dead *again* in the Broken Desert. That's Warclaw. I can't beat him."

"We have to run," Illium said.

"Run?" Vail asked. "Into battle, or away from it? It's not like you to run from a necessary conflict, Illium."

"Forgive me, my prince, but that thing tore off my legs and ripped my body to shreds. Looking at him now, I actually feel pain in my prosthetics. Perhaps we *should* stay and fight, but I, regrettably, may be of no use in this battle; for I am *frozen* with fear."

Drae Shivvan groaned, as he and Quickwing peered into the dungeon through the vents. He backed up, putting a hand to the burning mark on his arm.

"What is it, Shivvan?" Quickwing asked.

"It's my … wound. The pain has come back. It will soon overtake me, and the pills that the priestess gave me are back in my quarters."

Quickwing studied the elf, assessing him. He nodded. "I understand. Celestian warriors have a breathing technique—"

Drae cried out, as a wave of pain coursed through him.

Quickwing peered through the vents. The robots were looking towards them. They began to approach. "Drae, we're discovered. We have to move."

The elf cried out again. He took in a deep breath. "You have to leave me. I can't go on."

"But you must."

"Even if I tried, I couldn't move fast enough. Better they take just me than both of us. Whatever good comes from this surveillance of ours, it's all up to you now, Quickwing. Stay in touch with Joryn."

Quickwing simply stared, unwilling to abandon his friend.

"Go!" Drae lowered his voice, "Escape, now, so that these brutes think I was acting alone. It's our *only* chance."

The grate began to come loose, as one of the robots tugged it from the wall.

Quickwing nodded, sadly, and crawled on without the brave Highland Elf. *I will do what I can*, he thought.

If only I had my wings.

The robots pulled the elf forcefully from the ventilation shaft and threw him to the ground.

"Drae Shivvan: identified. How many are you?" asked the lead robot.

Remembering their alleged stupidity, Drae answered, "How many do you see here?"

"One."

"Quite right, because I am alone." Drae cried out again and doubled over in pain.

As two of the other robots began breaking a larger hole in the wall, to investigate further, the lead robot said, "This one is alone. Do not waste your energy. Take him to the dungeon with the others."

The robots complied, dragging the prisoner off. If he hadn't been in such agony, Drae would surely have laughed at how easy it had been to manipulate his mechanical captors.

"Illium, you're trembling." Joryn dismounted his noble steed and patted him on the shoulder. "You've lived a thousand years, Illium. You'll not fall today. I swear it. Go now, into the Spiritwood Forest."

"But, Joryn … How can I abandon you?"

"You must. It is an order from your prince. So long as you live, I will have hope for the future. Go now. You are no use to anyone frozen with fear, and it is well understood to be frightened senseless when facing the monster who did *this* to you." He nodded, indicating Illium's bionic prosthetics.

"My prince …"

"Go, Illium. I command it. To remain now would be a defiance of the Imperial Blood, and you would be committing treason, punishable by death. Be gone!"

A tear rolled down the unicorn's cheek. He looked to Charger and the Unitron. "Son, Lance, you must avoid the creature's claws at *all* costs. Stay out of his reach, whatever you do. If he gets hold of you, there is nothing you can do."

"I will, Father," Charger said.

"Affirmative," Lance said. "Suggested strategy applied to tactics."

"Now go," Charger said. "We'll be all right."

Illium nodded, continuing to weep with shame, and he turned to obey his prince, heading at a run towards the Spritwood Forest.

"Enough!" Vail shouted. "We must save the city! Lance! Into battle!"

"Command acknowledged." The Unitron reared up and charged towards the crab-like Warclaw.

"Vail," Joryn shouted after him, "don't!"

"Don't worry, I'm on it," Kail assured him and charged into battle himself, leaving Joryn behind without a steed.

Joryn looked to some of the people. "Water! Get to the wells! We need to put out the fires as quickly as they start! If you *follow* the robots, you aren't *technically* getting in their way."

The men and women nodded and sprang into action. Joryn watched the robots burning the buildings, knowing his command had been a feeble one, but hoping it would give the people something to do other than helplessly watch their homes burn to the ground.

"Vail!" Kail shouted. "Remember to avoid his—*Vail*!"

Warclaw swung his mighty claws at Lance, who was just out of range. The claws passed by Vail's face, his dark hair blowing in the gust created by the near blow.

"Now, Lance, in and out we go. Fire stun rays!"

Lance bolted closer to the creature and hit him with stun beams from both of his body cannons.

Warclaw looked down and laughed.

"It didn't work! Move!" Vail commanded.

Lance started to run, but it was too late. Warclaw's enormous left claw came down at them and knocked Lance into the air. The section of the Unitron's back directly beneath Vail shot up on a spring and launched the prince away before the robotic unicorn hit the ground several yards away.

Kail and Charger raced to Vail's aid. The younger man was already getting to his feet. They looked to Lance, who was likewise standing up.

The sprung panel on the Unitron's back lowered back down to its customary position, locking into place. "Damage assessment: negligible. Combat assessment: ready."

"Excellent, Lance! Then let us return to glorious battle!"

"Vail, wait!" Kail put a hand on his brother's shoulder. "We need a strategy. Rushing in like that almost got you killed."

"Standing around will not do us much better." Vail's eyes went wide. "Move!"

Charger and Vail jumped to either side of the descending claw, and it broke the ground with ease where they had been standing.

Joryn ran to join them then.

"Joryn, we're outmatched," Kail said urgently. "Get out of here! You can't move fast enough without a steed!"

Charger reared up and fell backwards, frantic to dodge the oncoming assault of the creature's mighty claw once again.

At the same instant, Warclaw saw his chance and swung his claw directly at the youngest prince.

"*Joryn*!" As Kail fell from Charger's saddle, he lost sight of the terrible event, his brother standing right beneath the oncoming, lethal claw of the monster.

There was a loud clang, and Kail was sure that his brother was dead. He got to his feet, just as Charger did, and found himself amazed.

There stood Joryn, his sword in one hand, and his shield raised above him upon the other arm, effortlessly holding off the massive demigod's claw.

Though he was just as surprised by the outcome of his own reflexive action, Joryn spoke as though he had expected it, "When last we met, Warclaw, I was only a boy. Now I am the champion of Libran. So face me, man to man, here and now, if you will. But do not expect me to fail against your might as I did before."

Warclaw lifted his claw, enraged, but cautious. He saw that the exoskeleton of his claw had been cracked, and the sight of it brought to his attention that it was throbbing with pain. "Gor'borgs! Priority one! Execute Joryn of Nod!" Warclaw slinked back, laughing. "You cannot raise a shield all night, little prince. Champion of Libran or not, you will tire, as my robot apes *never* do."

"Execute!"

"Execute Joryn of Nod!"

"Execute the twelfth-born pretender!"

Joryn raised his shield again, deflecting the incoming laser blasts.

Kail, having returned to Charger's saddle, rode by and snatched Joryn up, seating him on the unicorn's back in front of him. "Fall back, Vail!"

"Oh, so it's okay for you to say it!" Joryn shouted in jest.

"We had to move. Warclaw is right. The robots will overpower you. They'll overpower all of us."

Vail and Lance rode up beside them. "So, back to the old plan then?" Vail asked. "Joryn runs ahead, and I throw the shield?"

"No," Joryn said. "Not while Warclaw is out there. The robots may be stupid, but he can give them new orders. He would have them turn and wipe out the townspeople this time."

Taking a position behind a low wall, the princes dismounted, and their steeds crouched down. "We have to come up with a *new* strategy." Joryn sighed.

"Nice move with the shield, by the way," Vail said. "Told you it was magical."

"Message incoming," Lance announced.

"Joryn!"

"I'm here, Miiko. What news do you have?"

"Shivvan has been captured. I'm on my own now. How soon do you think you can get here?"

"I'm sorry, Miiko. We can't get to you at all now. Things have escalated here. It is we who need *your* help."

"But what can I do?"

"How heavily guarded is the dungeon?"

"There are a few robots in there. None of the other brute warriors."

"You have to get *our* warriors free, Miiko. Then get them to the Fighter Discs. We're overwhelmed out here. We *need* reinforcements."

"But, my prince, I am wounded. My wings … I am certain I cannot do this on my own."

A barrage of laser fire blew a chunk from the wall beside Joryn's head. Kail, Vail, and the equines were already creeping back, searching for further shelter. "Miiko … You *must*!"

Joryn rolled out of the way, as the wall came down. He stood and deflected another onslaught of laser fire with his shield and sword, as he backed off into the shadows. At least, for now, the townspeople had ceased to be targets. He took solace in that, but he knew that if he fell, the robots would turn back to the task of burning down the city and killing all who stood in their way.

Miiko Quickwing lay back in the ventilation shaft. The connection with Joryn had been lost. "I can't do it," he assured himself aloud. Tucking the communicator back into his belt, he tried to flex his wings, winced again. "I'm nothing without my wings."

He remembered the sound of desperation that had been in Joryn's voice. "But I *must*." He shook his head, then perked up with an idea. "They're stupid. But are they *that* stupid?" He smirked. "It's worth a try. If not, at least I'll go down fighting." He began to crawl towards an exit near the dungeon.

He removed the vent and stepped out into the hallway, walking down the stairs into the dungeon, sighting the robots. Only three of them, standing guard outside the prison bars that held all of the captives. Two cells. One for the royal family and the disciples of Joryn, and one for the palace guards, priests, and other servants who had been rounded up by the villains.

Quickwing walked confidently up to the robots, clearing his throat. "You there, I am here for the inspection."

"I have no orders regarding an inspection," said the first robot.

The second robot chimed in, scanning the new arrival. "Quickwing of Celestia: identified. Capture! Imprison!"

Quickwing laughed, as all three robots raised their laser rifles, pointing them right at him. "No, no, my good men. You are mistaken. I am the inspector."

The third robot spoke. "No. We are not mistaken. You are Quickwing of Celestia, defender of the false empire. Ally to Joryn of Nod."

"No, no. I only look *similar* to Quickwing of Celestia. I get that all the time. No, I was sent here by your master to inspect the prisoners. Scan me again. You'll see. Note this bandage across my chest. Does Quickwing of Celestia have such a bandage? Search your databanks."

"No bandage on file image of Quickwing of Celestia," said the first robot.

"And look at me closer. I'm covered in dust! Is there dust on your file image of Quickwing?"

"No dust," the second robot agreed.

"So what is your conclusion then? How could I be Quickwing of Celestia, if I do not *match* your file image of him?"

The robots considered.

"Now go back just a few moments. Check your databanks on *me*, on who I said I was when I entered the room. Do your databank images of the dusty, bandaged inspector who approached you then match the Celestian you see standing here before you now?"

"Affirmative," the third robot said. "Conclusion: you are *not* Quickwing of Celestia. You are the inspector."

"The inspector brings orders from the Wanderer. He must inspect the prisoners." The first robot turned to the second. "Unlock Cell Unit One for the inspector."

"Acknowledged."

"Thank you," Quickwing said, as the robot unlocked the cell. He looked to the first robot. "Now, I will need to use your gun. To test their reflexes."

"Acknowledged."

The robot handed its gun to Quickwing, who wasted no time in shooting its head right off. He turned, before the other two robots could process the change in their circumstances, and he shot their heads off in quick succession as well. He saw Longshot about to crow out with joy, and he put a finger to his lips, reminding the prisoners that there were far more than three robots remaining in the palace.

Quickwing opened the cell door, speaking urgently, "Joryn's in the city, fighting more of those robots alongside the townspeople. He needs reinforcements desperately. If we're going to take back the palace *and* save the city, we need to get to the new Fighter Discs." He looked over the soon-to-be former inmates of Cell Unit One. All of the elite warriors were accounted for and combat ready, save for Drae Shivvan, who lay hunched over in pain against the far wall. The royal family was there, except for Joryn, Kail, and Vail. Tianna and Iron Bill were trapped in a separate cage within the cell, which appeared to be made entirely out of a solid green light. He opened his mouth to question it but was stopped by an answer from the priestess.

"Don't bother with Iron Bill and me. This magical cage will stand as long as the twin sorcerers who created it are able to concentrate their powers. There's nothing you can do here and now, so whatever you have planned, you'll have to leave us out of the equation."

Quickwing nodded. "All right then." He looked to the emperor, who was conscious, but clearly weakened. "Your Majesty, I recommend that you and your family stay here until the battle is through. I can think of no safer place." He removed his sword from its sheath at his side and cut through the ropes that bound Kabed's arms and legs, then did the same for Longshot.

Kabed and Longshot began freeing the others of their bonds.

Longshot unbound Trig, who switched immediately back to his horse form, shaking off the feeling of helplessness that had come over him from being trapped in gun form and aimed down from the wall at his best friend. Longshot laughed. "That's right, shake it off, buddy."

Kabed untied Onri Sprigg and Lowgun, who in turn began helping to free the others. Meanwhile, Quickwing took the keys from one of the fallen robots to the cell next door and released the palace guards, who had been paying close attention to what was going on in Cell Unit One.

Longshot unbound Princess Hero and gave her a wink. "Told you I'd save you, Princess."

She rolled her eyes and shook her head with a mixture of irritation and amusement. "My hero," she said sarcastically.

As the guards joined them outside the cells, Quickwing looked to Starro.

Starro deferred to him. "So what's the plan, Quickwing? My guards are at your disposal."

Stunned at the implication, that the captain of the Guard saw him as having assumed command and so readily accepted it, Quickwing nodded. "If I may be so bold, Captain Starro, I would suggest you take half of your guards and help Kabed, Equus, and Sprigg get to the Fighter Discs. Kabed will know how to fly them. Meanwhile, if the other half will accompany me, Longshot, and Lowgun into the heart of the palace, we will take it back by force. We weren't ready for these monsters when they hit us, but we are ready now." He threw the robot's laser rifle that he had taken to Starro. "We have, at present, three guns among us, my sword, and of course Trig. Every robot we fell gives us another gun."

He looked to Kabed. "When you get to the Fighter Discs, get as many in the air as you can. Send half to the city to help Joryn. The rest should stay here and help mop up these villains. These robots are nothing but stupid, lifeless instruments of war, and the organic warriors are nothing against those Fighter Discs. I've seen the Whispering Plains' aircraft in action before."

Kabed and Captain Starro both nodded.

"Sounds like a plan," Kabed said with a grin.

"Yeah," Princess Hero said drily. "It's a *great* plan, if it doesn't get you all killed."

"Hey, you're coming too, right?" Longshot nudged her with his elbow. "I know what you can bring to a fight."

"Oh, I wouldn't miss it," Hero said with her customary scofflaw grin.

"I'm coming too," Prince Dorago said, matter-of-factly.

Hero nodded, approving.

"Not on your life!" Sapros shouted with all of his diminished strength. "You are both staying put and waiting the battle out right here."

"But, Father—"

"I have *spoken*, Hero! You are my children, and that makes you the perfect hostages if one of you is wounded or captured out there. These terrorists could take you and make demands of me, and if I didn't negotiate on your behalf the people of the Empire would think me heartless. I'll not be put in that position. You're staying here."

Hero and Dorago exchanged a look.

"I'm grateful for your concern, Father," Hero said with an unmistakable edge of bitterness in her voice.

"Hero," Willowyll put a hand on her shoulder gently, and softly said, "mind your tone."

Emperor Sapros simply glared at the two of them.

"All right then," Quickwing said. "There's nothing more than to set out." He looked to Kabed and Starro. "Good luck."

"Same to you," Kabed said, picking up one of the laser guns. "Lasers," he scoffed. "So much messier than our light rays."

"They'll do the job," Starro said.

"Oh, they will indeed," Kabed agreed. "I'm not afraid of making a mess."

Kail's wife, Princess Maressah, approached Quickwing quietly. "Has there been any word of my husband?"

"None, my lady, but I'm sure he's all right. He may even be with Joryn in the city. You know he's brave and clever. I wouldn't worry."

She nodded, pretending to agree that worry was the furthest thing from her mind.

"And what of the other provinces?" Dorran Equus asked him then. "Golan says they were all hit at the same time we were." The tremor of barely contained fear in his voice was unmistakable. "My son, Lute, has been visiting his grandparents among the centaurs."

Quickwing put a hand on the centaur's shoulder. "We all have loved ones back home whom we are worried about, Equus. The sooner we retake the palace and get communications back online, the sooner all of our hearts will be relieved by their well-being."

The centaur puffed out his broad chest and looked determinedly into the Celestian's eyes. "Then let us get to it and live or die as heroes of the realm."

Quickwing smiled, loving the centaur for his courage in the midst of his fear.

As the warriors moved out of the dungeon, Captain Starro went into the first cell. Having no concern left for the scandal he might cause, he approached Willowyll.

She shook her head, subtly, attempting to dissuade him.

He smiled, defiant, and took her in his arms, just as he had in the garden, kissing her passionately for all to see.

Desperately in love with him, Willowyll could not help but give in. "Captain," she said at last, "you amaze me."

"You give me my courage, and every reason to succeed," Starro replied.

The stunned silence of the onlookers was palpable, broken only by Prince Repteré's scathing comment, "Oh like you didn't *all* already know."

Nervous laughter followed from the others. All except for Willowyll's father, the king, who glared murder at the captain of the Guard.

Starro nodded to his second. "Lieutenant Moon, lead your half of the Guard and follow Quickwing into the palace. We'll split into training teams. Group A with me, Group B with you."

Lieutenant Moon nodded soberly. "Your will is our command, Captain Starro."

"May the gods go with us," Starro began the battle mantra of the Imperial Guard.

Moon smiled, finishing the phrase, "And may we honor them with our victory."

The two groups went their separate ways, each very slowly and craftily taking down enough of the robot soldiers to arm themselves and move on towards their ultimate goals.

"I grow tired of this waiting!" the Wanderer growled. "Dreadfin, see if you can raise Warclaw through the Gor'borgs' communicators. I want a status report. How long can it possibly take to carry out my will against three foolish, spoiled princes?"

"Right away, Master," the fingrin said, gnashing his metal teeth nervously. He knew what happened when the Wanderer grew impatient, and he was loath to be so near to him when his temper went out of control.

"Target the robots, then hit the throne!" Quickwing shouted, as his team entered the audience chamber.

Laser beams began flying, hitting the robots unprepared.

"Gor'borgs!" Dreadfin commanded, "Defend the Wanderer!"

"Defend!" the robots began to parrot.

But it was too little, too late. Most of the robots had already fallen before the fingrin's command had come.

Sizing up the number of guards and warriors who were filing into the room, the Wanderer began planning his escape. "Gemino, Gemina! Help Dreadfin and the Gor'borgs to destroy these insolent rebels! Razorwing! Jakknife! Come with me!"

Three of the guards fell to the rifles of the remaining robot apes, and Lieutenant Moon was quick to exact revenge on the mechanical soldiers, blasting them all right through their tiny, electronic brains and watching them fall.

The fingrin snarled. "You may have numbers on your side for the moment, but we have all the powers of darkest sorcery!"

"Sorry, Dreadfin," Gemina said, noting that the Wanderer had already left them behind.

"Too many of them to mess with," Gemino finished for her.

The twins put their hands together and vanished in a ball of light.

"Cowards!" Dreadfin shouted. He growled, showing his full collection of mechanized teeth to his enemies.

Having refrained from utilizing Trig's gun form for the sake of discretion as they made their way to the throne room, Longshot pointed his purloined laser rifle at the shark man. "Stow it, Teeth. Looks like you're *our* prisoner now."

"Not before I take off your head, buckaroo!" Dreadfin ran at Longshot, jaws wide open and ready for the kill.

"Trig! Switch! Set for stun!" Longshot dropped his laser rifle, knowing that it would be a violation of his pledge to Joryn if he were to use it on a living enemy.

The horse managed the transformation just before the creature reached Longshot, and he knocked the fingrin back with a close-range stun blast that might have killed him regardless, had he been born of a less sturdy species.

The reptisaur Lowgun went forward, carrying some rope he'd brought with him from the dungeon, and he bound Dreadfin's hands and feet, just to be sure. He looked to Quickwing. "I think that does it, boss. One more impossible mission accomplished."

Quickwing nodded, flexing his wings, feeling the pain in his chest as a badge of honor now, rather than an impediment. He had earned the wound through his heroism, and he had remained a hero in spite of it. "Yes. 'Impossible,' Lowgun, is solely a state of mind. Now let's just hope Kabed's team has been as successful."

"What about that guy with the crazy head gear?" Longshot asked.

"The so-called *Wanderer*," Quickwing said. "He ran off with that revolting Chirop and another of his henchmen." He turned to Lieutenant Moon. "Secure the throne room. Stand ready for *any* attack until we *know* the enemy forces have been driven fully from the palace."

To Lowgun, he said, "When it's safe, bring the emperor back here to send a message to the people of the realm that the enemy has been defeated. If there are similar battles raging across our lands, it will give them encouragement and add to their fighting spirit until we can send them any aid."

He turned to the gunslinger. "Longshot, he went that way."

Together, Quickwing and Longshot followed the trail of the Wanderer back into the palace.

"Execute Joryn of Nod!"

Joryn raised his shield to fend off yet another barrage of laser fire.

"We're out of places to run," Kail said.

"Then we make our last stand a magnificent one!" Vail crowed, raising his sword into the air. "Come, robot monkeys! If the emperor's sons must die, then let us die together!"

"Not the option I had in mind," Kail said.

Joryn glanced back, rolling his eyes at Vail's dramatics. He then turned his attention back to the approaching line of robots and threw his shield, mowing them down.

"Bad timing, Joryn!" Kail shouted.

The second line of robots opened fire, and Joryn deftly blocked the blasts with his sword until the shield returned to his hand. "I think I'm getting the hang of this magic weapon thing." He laughed.

"You're acting like Vail, Little Brother."

"Yes," Vail said. "Our little brother takes quickly to the art of battle." He grinned. "Which you, I know, have no true heart for."

"My battles are better fought with a sharp tongue than with a sword," Kail agreed. "Open warfare is not my arena."

Vail nodded. "And Joryn has grown to match us *both* now in either arena."

"Oh, stop it," Joryn said. "You both learned everything you know from *me*. End of discussion. New topic: how do we get out of this?"

Charger reared up and kicked at the wall behind them with his hind legs. "Too sturdy."

"We could let some of the laser blasts slip past," Vail suggested, "knock the wall down *for* us."

"Negative," Lance cautioned. "The wall is strong, but structurally imperative. If destroyed, the entire building will collapse."

"Then our legends will be born here at our deaths, our magnificent—"

"Shut up, Vail! This is serious!" Kail snapped.

"You think I wasn't being serious?"

"Execute!" The robots unleashed another barrage directly at the youngest prince.

Blocking the laser blasts once again, Joryn turned his head in a huff to his bickering brothers. "Well, *I'm* all out of ideas here, and I can't keep using the shield like this. My arms are wearing out." He threw the shield again, repeating his performance from moments before.

"Enough of this!" Warclaw commanded at last. The robots parted, allowing him to walk forward. "The Wanderer wants you dead, Prince Joryn, and I have no desire to report a failure or even a delay. So here is your choice." He held up his claws, a young boy from the city in one, a young girl in the other, both in tears from sheer terror. "Surrender now, come forward, and die … or I will snap these two young citizens of the Imperial city in half." His eyes narrowed. "And you *know* I will do as I say. You know from experience." The demigod grinned poisonously at the young hero.

"How do I know you'll let them go if I surrender?"

Warclaw only continued to smile. "Is that a yes, or a no?" He began to squeeze, and his captives cried out in pain.

"I surrender!" Joryn threw down his weapons without hesitation, though his brothers were quick to tighten their grips on their own. "I surrender, Warclaw. You win. Now let them go."

Warclaw laughed. "Heroes are so predictable."

"Then you should have seen *this* coming, monster," a voice rang out from behind the demigod.

Warclaw turned. "You! How many times must I kill you before you'll die?"

"Illium!" Joryn was amazed at his friend's courage. "What are you doing?"

"What I must, my prince." The green status lights near Illium's gun turrets changed to red.

"Illium, no!"

"Trust me, my prince."

"Your little toy guns are nothing to my armor, unicorn." Warclaw tossed his captives aside, snapping his deadly pincers menacingly in Illium's direction. "Do allow me to remind you."

As Warclaw approached, Illium stood his ground.

"Illium, run!" Joryn pleaded, he retrieved his sword and shield from the ground, then noticed that the status lights on

Lance's weapons had changed from green to red as well. "Lance, what are you doing? You can't kill him!"

"Affirmative." Lance nodded to Illium.

Illium's eyes smiled, as Warclaw prepared to smite the unicorn a third time.

Illium opened fire, pummeling the demigod from the front.

Lance opened fire as well, hitting him from the other side.

Joryn lunged forward to stop them, but his brothers held him back.

"Sometimes, Joryn," Kail said, "there's just no other way to win."

"This isn't winning," Joryn said, brokenheartedly.

Illium stopped, and Lance followed suit.

Warclaw swooned. "Yyyyyou … have … nnnnot …"

"It's like he's drunk," Vail said. "What is this, Lance?"

"If stun beams do not stun him, kill beams do not kill him. However—"

"They may *stun* him!" Joryn was elated.

"… wwwwon." Warclaw reached out, as he fell, and grabbed hold of one of Illium's legs.

Illium whinnied in terror.

"Not on your life!" Joryn ran straight for the monster and right up the shell of his back. He sheathed his sword, raised his shield, and swung with all of his might, smacking the crab-like demigod across the back of the skull.

Warclaw fell.

Joryn leapt from the monster's shoulders, ran to his unicorn friend, and hugged him. "Illium! You did it! We defeated him at last! I'm so glad you came back."

"I had no intention of hiding in the forest, my prince. I simply had to collect my courage."

"I should have known."

"Um, guys?" Kail brought them back to the matter at hand. "The battle's not over."

"What are your orders?" one of the Gor'borgs asked the unconscious Warclaw.

"That is true," Vail said, as they all assessed the perplexed robots. "But it *is* completely stupid."

The robots continued to look at each other, until one of them said, "Execute Joryn of Nod!"

"Right." Joryn laughed. "So, back to Vail's favorite plan." He threw the shield to his brother, swung himself up onto Illium's back, and drew full attention to his identity. "Come and get me, apes! I am Joryn of Nod!"

Illium took off running, the young prince on his back, and several of the robots followed.

"Execute!" the robots began to parrot.

"Execute the twelfth-born prince!"

Vail caught the shield, a wide grin spreading across his face. "I really do love this strategy with the stupid-bots." He mounted his mechanical steed and looked to his older brother. "Do the honors?"

"With pleasure." Kail, now back in Charger's saddle, raised his sword. "People of Imperial City! Return to arms! Warclaw has fallen! Victory *will* be ours!"

And then he heard another of the robots say, "Burn the city! Kill any who get in the way!"

A group of the warrior machines broke away from those following Joryn and Illium and began repeating, "Burn the city!"

"Um, Kail," Vail said, "I think we have a problem."

"You think?" Kail shook his head with an agitated sigh. "This is your arena, Brother. So, what are we waiting for?" He patted Charger on the shoulders. "Into the fray."

Charger ran towards the robots, carrying Kail.

"You heard the man, Lance!"

"Affirmative." The Unitron followed Charger, the two brothers determined to take down as many of the enemy soldiers as they could.

Back at the palace, Kabed and Starro's group reached the landing field, where they found the new Fighter Discs, as well as the Wanderer's own aircraft. "That is one ugly sky ship," Kabed said, assessing the *Darkstar*.

"Fitting for that festering mound of steaming poopie called the Wanderer," Onri agreed.

"Let's wreck it," Dorran Equus suggested, kicking his hind legs back eagerly.

"No time," Kabed said. "Starro, have you lined up our pilots?"

"Already getting onboard their craft and assigned to battle groups. Four will be following us into the city, while the other five will focus on cleaning off the rest of the robots here at the palace. It was serendipitous to have so many in the ranks who come from the Whispering Plains and already know these craft."

Kabed nodded. "Then let's go. You're with me, Starro. Dorran, Onri, each of you fly with a different group. Clean off the rest of the enemy robots from the palace, then return here to be sure the Wanderer doesn't escape in his own craft."

Captain Starro called to two of his men, "Jesstra, Pim, stand guard in front of that monstrous thing. If that villain dares to run back here, stun him on sight. He should never even get into the air." He gave them a reassuring nod. "This will all be over soon."

"Yes, Sir!" the men said, obeying immediately.

As Kabed and Starro boarded the Fighter Disc, followed by several of the guards, and Kabed began firing up the engines, Starro noticed something hanging at the tech wizard's side. "When did you pick up *that* thing?"

"My glue gun? I found it on the ground just before we got to the hangar. Didn't want to leave it."

"Yeah, it would be so awful if that advanced Deluvian tech fell into enemy hands."

"Mock me, Starro. But you'll see. There will yet be a use for the … Trapper … Thing."

"Maybe, if you ever think up an appropriate name for it."

"I assure you, I will." Kabed raised the boarding ramp, sealed the hatchway, and lifted the craft into the air easily; the other Fighter Discs following him into the air.

Kabed flew his own disc away, towards the city, followed by four other of the vehicles. He noted on the viewscreens that the remaining robots at the palace had taken to the air with their jetpacks and were engaging the other group of Fighter Discs in battle. Stupid as the robots had proven to be, he had no doubt that the battle would fall in favor of his friends.

***

"Joryn," Vail called out. "This isn't working!" He used Joryn's shield to block two laser rifle assaults from the oncoming robots.

"I can see that!" Joryn and Illium had just made a circle around a city block, barely evading the laser bolts that the robots had been firing at their backs. Vail had been unable to let go of the shield, having had attackers of his own to defend against. "Illium, turn and attack."

The unicorn spun around, opened the panels at his sides, and once again unleashed the Deluvian light guns he had been equipped with. He fired into the horde of robot soldiers, as Joryn blocked their shots with his sword. "There are just too many of them."

Watching the robots move in on them from all sides, Joryn nodded. "Yeah, but we're not going to let them take us down easily."

Just then, five Fighter Discs flew onto the scene and started firing down at the robots, quickly clearing a path for Joryn's escape. The lead disc lowered, and Captain Starro leapt out, along with a group of palace guards, joining in the ground battle with their stolen laser guns, just as a significant number of the Gor'borgs ignited their jetpacks and engaged the other four Fighter Discs in the air.

"Starro!" Vail greeted the leader of the guards. "Great timing, my friend!" He held out his sword with a shrug. The three of us only brought our swords to this laser fight."

Starro nodded. "We're here now. You said three. Is Prince Kail here as well?"

Joryn and Illium rode up to them then. "He's gone to help battle the fires. The robots have gone in all directions. We took out their commander, and mass chaos ensued." He nodded towards the unconscious demigod.

"Fantastic!" Starro laughed. "While I remain unconvinced that you needed any help, we are here to serve you."

Joryn nodded with a smile. "Then let's clean this mess up!"

With the arrival of the Imperial Guard and Kabed, and with their multitude of confiscated laser guns, the battle on the ground was quickly won.

CHAPTER 9:
IN PURSUIT OF THE *DARKSTAR*

THE WANDERER WALKED OUT ONTO THE LANDING FIELD, flanked by Razorwing and Jakknife. Behind his inhuman mask, he sneered at the sight of the two guards standing at the entrance to his aircraft.

The two men raised their guns.

"Halt!" commanded the guard called Jesstra. He looked to his comrade, Pim, in doubt, as the three enemies' strides failed to even slow.

Pim pointed his laser rifle directly at the Wanderer. "Stop right there, or we *will* open fire! You are under arrest, in the name of the—"

A quick blast from one of the many armaments concealed within Jakknife's body seared directly into Pim's chest and silenced him forever.

Horrified, Jesstra opened fire on the three villains.

"Mine," the Wanderer said simply. He began to spin his staff, as he'd done before, creating a shield that easily deflected the rays of the guardsman's gun.

As the Wanderer drew close to him, Jesstra shouted in disbelief, "What *are* you?"

The Wanderer, now within range to do so, abruptly raised his spinning staff and allowed it to slice cleanly through the neck of the guardsman. Watching the man's silently screaming head fall to the ground with a sickening thud, he answered coldly, "Ask your gods." He raised the staff above his own head then and silently beckoned the boarding ramp of the *Darkstar* to lower. The Wanderer boarded without further delay, followed by his henchmen.

"There they are!" Quickwing shouted, walking onto the landing field too late.

Longshot fired at the craft with Trig, but barely scratched the exterior of the rising ramp.

Jakknife got off two shots, neither of which found their mark, just before the ramp sealed the villains into the Wanderer's vessel.

The *Darkstar* lifted off, deep purple lights all over its steel hull coming to life. It rose above the palace walls and sped away, carrying the instigator of all the day's unforgivable terrors to freedom.

Quickwing spoke urgently into an open channel on his communicator. "All Fighter Discs, the Wanderer is in the air! Repeat: the Wanderer is in the air!"

Kabed stood at the ramp of his Fighter Disc in Imperial City, having just received the message from the palace. "I just heard from Quickwing. The Wanderer has escaped them and taken to the sky."

Joryn and Starro stood at the foot of the ramp, catching their breath after the battle. The other princes and many of the guards were assisting in putting out the few fires that still burned, and the citizens had gathered enough chains to keep Warclaw in place if he awoke before being transferred to a proper prison cell at the palace.

"Damn it," Starro said. "I hate to think of that *monster* escaping from justice. So many people died today." He clenched his fists in anger.

"We may yet bring him to justice, Starro!" Joryn pointed to the sky. "*That* is not one of our Fighter Discs."

"No, it's not," Starro agreed.

The two men rushed up the ramp, past Kabed.

"What are you waiting for, Kabed?" Joryn asked. "We have to go after him!"

Kabed nodded and followed them into the battle craft, closing the ramp behind them and taking to the air.

As they pursued the *Darkstar*, Kabed noticed on the viewscreens that several more discs had headed after the Wanderer from the palace, only to be blocked by another slew of the flying robots. "How many of those robot apes do they *have*?"

"Too many," Joryn answered. "But they are easily beaten. The other fighters will catch up."

"We're in range," Kabed announced.

"We need to slow him down," Joryn said. "If you take out one of his engines, will he still be able to stay airborne?"

"I don't know the design of his craft, but from the look of it, I'd say he has engine power to spare."

"Then do it. Fire!"

Kabed launched a salvo of light rays from the Fighter Disc at the *Darkstar*, but the craft deftly dodged each shot. "He's a good pilot. Whoever's flying that thing."

"Keep trying, Kabed. We *have* to take this villain down."

Kabed nodded and continued to fire at the enemy craft to no avail.

On board the *Darkstar*, the Wanderer growled. "Return fire, Razorwing. Destroy whatever fool has dared to give us chase!"

At the helm, Razorwing nodded and fired the rear laser cannons. He snarled in frustration. "Energy shields. I think the tech is Deluvian. Our lasers won't get through."

"Bah! We have *stupid* robots, we have *weak* firepower! I apparently need to get a Deluvian tech wizard of my own before we strike next." He punched the wall of the cockpit, denting it. "When did the Deluvians start *sharing* their technological wonders with the Empire?"

"The Imperial palace acquired a tech wizard about five years ago," Razorwing said. "But I didn't know they had advanced so much. When they invaded Chiroptera, they had light guns, a handful of flight packs, and a single mechanical horse. There was no indication the emperor had any sort of sky fighter craft like these."

Jakknife spoke up, the red light of his single robotic eye fluctuating with his vocal cadence. "I can take out their shields, Master."

The Wanderer laughed. "Yes. Of course you can! Go then, Jakknife. We will knock them out of the sky yet."

"Either way," Jakknife said, "I doubt they have the capacity to follow us all the way back to Mount Dread."

"Go!" the Wanderer barked.

Jakknife bowed his head and left the cockpit.

"What is that?" Starro asked, pointing at the screen.

"It's that mechanical menace Jakknife," Kabed answered. "Apparently, he can fly. And he's headed right for us." He fired at the enemy, but Jakknife dodged.

"Do you want me to man the guns, Kabed?" Starro offered.

"It's not my *aim*, Captain. I would have hit him *and* that ugly air ship if they would just stay still."

"Where did he go?" Joryn asked.

"He's right on top of us," Kabed answered, grimly. "Get ready. There's no way that walking, talking armory isn't going to board us."

Starro and Joryn ran into the main cargo hold of the craft, just as a diamond-blade saw began cutting through the hull from the outside.

Jakknife pushed aside the cut metal and walked casually into the Fighter Disc, the outside energy shield containing the air pressure within. "Greetings, fools." He fired at them, missing as they dived out of the way, knocking more holes in the other side of the craft. Ultimately unconcerned with them, Jakknife scanned the Fighter Disc and located the source of the shields. He turned and quickly blasted the generator with a light gun from his arm, then continued scanning.

As the energy shield went out, the craft was instantly depressurized, and everything that wasn't locked down began flying out through the breach.

Joryn grabbed hold of a seat strap along the wall, and Starro grabbed hold of Joryn.

Jakknife laughed at the precariously placed heroes. "Oh, this is too easy!"

"Hold it, Jakknife!" Kabed said, as he walked in from the cockpit. "You're not the only one with magnetic armor."

Jakknife looked the Deluvian tech wizard up and down, scanning his armor and noting the strange gun that was now aimed directly at his chest. "Oh, please. As if you posed any real threat to—"

The robot's words were cut off by a blast that rocked the entire craft. He laughed again. "It seems my master has taken full advantage of your decimated shields. I shall therefore leave you to your fates." Jakknife fired up his built-in rocket pack and lifted up from the ground.

Kabed pulled the trigger.

The robot yelped out in surprise as the dart's gluey strands wrapped themselves around him, pinning his arms and legs against his body. He fell to the floor with a clang and was immediately sucked out through the hole in the wall.

"*Kabed*!" Joryn shouted, still holding on to the seat straps for dear life.

Nodding once, Kabed ran back to the cockpit.

Another blast rocked the Fighter Disc.

Kabed frantically looked over the controls until he found the backup shield generator that he suspected to be there and activated it. He took the next instant to fire another shot at the unsuspecting enemy craft, scoring a direct hit on one of its four engines. He looked at the status of his own engines and sighed, realizing that they had effectively lost their quarry.

He ran back out to find Joryn and Starro regaining their footing.

Joryn gave his friend a bewildered look. "How did you—?"

"Backup generator," Kabed answered.

He looked to Starro and held up his invention. "I told you this thing would be useful."

Starro offered a wry smirk. "Even without a name."

"So, we have shields again?" Joryn took in the new situation. "And who's—?"

"Auto pilot," Kabed said. "I locked onto the Wanderer's ship. We're following it, but I'm afraid they got in a couple of pretty good shots before I restored the shield. We're never going to catch up with them. I even took out one of their engines when they thought we were dead in the air, but they did much worse damage to us."

Joryn looked behind him to three smaller, open aircraft that were parked inside the Fighter Disc. "What are those?"

"Cloud Skiffs," Kabed said. "They're like lifeboats, in case we need to abandon the Fighter Disc."

"Are they fast?"

"I don't know, but— Joryn, no! It's too much of a risk. You'll be open to the elements. No shields. Even if you *could* catch up—"

But Joryn was already climbing onto the closest Cloud Skiff and looking for the ignition switch. "Kabed, that *monster*, whoever he is, just *murdered* more people than I dare to imagine, all across the Empire if what Golan told you is true. I will *not* let him escape Imperial justice." He fired up the ignition.

"Joryn! You can't just jump into action like this all the time! The dragons steal your boyfriend, and you just ride off to get him back! You come back from Chiroptera and just tell your father off like he's nobody! All in the name of justice! But one day, it's going to come back and bite you in the—"

"Sorry, Kabed. I can't hear you over the sound of my own self-righteousness."

"You arrogant—!"

"You will not go into this battle alone," Captain Starro declared, cutting off the last of Kabed's protests, as he climbed into the skiff beside Nod's youngest prince. "Don't worry, Kabed. I have his back in this. And he's right. If there is even a *chance* that we can bring this villain in, we need to take it."

Joryn lifted the skiff off of the ground and moved towards the opening in the side of the Fighter Disc. "Keep following that air ship, Kabed. If we succeed, we'll need someone to come after us."

Sighing with resignation, Kabed said, "May Libran watch over you, my prince."

Joryn nodded his head with a confident smile, then flew the Cloud Skiff out into the open air.

Kabed watched them depart, shaking his head. "You're not indestructible, Joryn," he said to the deaf wind at the hero's back. "If you came back from Chiroptera thinking that you were, then you learned the wrong lesson. I hope that monster isn't the one to let you know it." He shook his head. "Now I'm talking to myself. Clearly crazy is contagious." He turned and went back to the cockpit, watching as Joryn closed in on the *Darkstar*, and as both craft flew ever farther into the distance before him.

In the cockpit of the *Darkstar*, Razorwing continued to fire at the little Cloud Skiff. "They're still gaining. It's Prince Joryn. He clearly has Libran's protection over him. I can't get a shot."

The Wanderer laughed derisively. "No. Libran is *not* with him. It's nothing more than luck. I have more of an understanding of the so-called gods than anyone. The only *protection* he has with him right now is an Imperial guardsman. Open the hatch."

"Master?"

"Don't worry, my magic will keep the vessel pressurized. I will face this bold new champion, and I will put an end to him before he can grow into a true threat."

"As you command, Master." Razorwing hit the control to open the hatch at the side, which was just large enough for the Cloud Skiff to dock.

Shouting over the wind, directly into Joryn's ear, Captain Starro voiced his concern, "They've stopped firing and opened the hatch. Clearly this is a trap. How do you want to proceed?"

"It may be a trap, but it's still our only chance at bringing the Wanderer in. I say we proceed bravely."

"I perfectly agree," Starro shouted.

Joryn brought the Cloud Skiff in for a landing, shutting the engines off abruptly as they docked in the *Darkstar's* hold and leaping from the vehicle with his sword and shield drawn, presumably ready for anything.

Starro did likewise, his finger ready at the trigger of his laser gun.

"No robot apes," Joryn observed.

"No one at all," Starro said.

The door to the cockpit opened, and a terrifying personage joined them in the main hold. "There is no one here, save for me and my pilot," the man said in a dark voice that echoed unnaturally within his monstrous mask.

Joryn gasped at the sight of him. The villain wore a threadbare gray robe, which concealed most of his body. In conjunction with the mask, it was impossible to determine the monster's species; and the mask itself was something out of a nightmare. It looked both lifeless and organic, with tendrils that looked like roots appearing to grow directly from the mask and right down into the man's body. There was a black, empty void where the man's eyes should have been, were he human, but the mask itself was so overwhelming that Joryn could not see the eyes within the darkness at all; not from the present distance between himself and this nightmarish enemy. And from the top of the mask sprouted a pair of antler-like horns. The mask looked equal parts dead and alive and may well have been the villain's only true face.

Joryn forced himself to recover from the sight, bolstering his own courage. *He's only one man,* he thought to himself. *You've faced down the queen of dragons, the armies of Chiroptera, and even the emperor of Nod himself. This is only one man, against two. There is nothing to fear.*

The man approached them then, the green three-headed serpent staff in his right hand beginning to glow. "Make no mistake. You *will* die, but I needed to see you for myself." He looked at the sword and shield in Joryn's hands. "So, it is true. You *do* bear the true Sword and Shield of my old enemy Libran."

"What do you know of Libran?" Joryn asked, angrily.

The Wanderer laughed. "I am the Wanderer of old. I have been in Nod as long as the gods themselves. I have long threatened the balance that your *divine* patron so cherishes. You are not the first warrior whom he has set against me. And you will not be the last. You will fall, as your predecessor did. But you will never have the opportunity to grow into the nemesis that he was. You are young and untempered. You will not survive this foolish attempt to bring me to justice."

"You're nothing but a madman," Starro shouted out. "The Wanderer was killed a thousand years ago, if he existed at all. He's a myth. And you are under arrest in the name of the Empire!"

The Wanderer laughed as though the captain of the Guard had been telling him a joke. "Oh, insolent pest. I have just told you that the one who bears the Sword and Shield of Libran is nothing to me. If that is so, then you are *less* than nothing."

"Captain Starro speaks the truth," Joryn said. "You can't be the Wanderer. Everyone who knows the myth knows that Palo killed the Wanderer a thousand years ago. And what of the legends of the Darkening Scourge? Yet another report of your death, at the hands of Bran's son, just before the Scourge was unleashed. If either *one* of those conflicting myths is true, then the Wanderer is very dead."

"Oh," the Wanderer said, "you will never gain the experience to know that there are some things that simply do not die. Can one kill murder itself? Can one kill guilt? Can one kill hunger? Can one kill vengeance? I *am* murder! I *am* hunger and despair! I *am* vengeance twice over! Bran may have put my plans on hold when he held the weapons you hold now, but I assure you, when his son unleashed his wrath upon me, he was destroyed in the process. As was the legendary hero Palo, who was said to have killed me last, but only found his own destruction at my hands!" He pulled back a portion of his robe to reveal an ancient breastplate. "I kept *this* as a memento of that magnificent battle."

Joryn recognized the symbol on the breastplate from his lessons with Parakletos. "The seal of Palo!"

"Any who have sought to destroy me have met their own dark destinies instead. And those were mighty men, seasoned by years of conflict. You are a boy who knows nothing of war; who knows nothing of Libran; and nothing of *me*! If I were capable, I might pity you for the death you will now suffer, for the legendary sword-bearer you will never grow to become."

"Enough! You are coming with us. We are armed, and you only have—"

A blast of green energy shot forth from the Wanderer's staff, and Joryn raised his shield just in time. The force still threw him back against the wall, knocking the wind from him.

The Wanderer approached Captain Starro with quick, determined strides.

"Stand down!" the captain shouted. "You are a prisoner of the emperor!"

When the Wanderer did not stop, Starro opened fire.

The Wanderer spun his staff, deflecting the shots. When he stood close enough, he knocked the gun from Starro's grasp with the back of his hand. Before Starro could respond, the Wanderer lunged forward, impaling the captain of the Guard through the chest with the end of his staff.

Starro looked down in shock, his voice having left him as he tried to cry out. The staff had gone all the way through him. He tried to reach for it, but his arms failed him.

"Behold the fate of *all* who love you, champion of Libran!" The Wanderer gripped his staff tighter, and its glow intensified.

Joryn, in perfect shock, rose to his feet, knowing that Starro's wound was fatal; knowing that he was powerless to save his friend; that he was powerless to save the love of Willowyll's life.

The staff glowed more brightly, and Captain Starro struggled helplessly, trying to cry out, as his body burned from within. In a terrible, crawling instant that seemed like forever, green flame shot out of Starro's mouth and eyes, incinerating him from the inside-out. Starro finally let out a mangled scream, and fell limp, his body continuing to burn on the staff.

The Wanderer unceremoniously chucked Captain Starro out through the open hatch, holding fast to his staff, as the broken body slid off of it, and turning to face the prince. "Less than nothing."

"*Starro*!" Joryn's heart was beating so hard that he feared it would fail within him. He had never seen such a terrible death. Aside from his mother, he had never lost any close friends; never in battle. "*No*!" He lunged at the Wanderer with his sword.

The Wanderer laughed devilishly, parrying the blow with his staff easily. "Yes! Do it! Dare to kill me! *Become* murder! *Become* vengeance! Still you will fail!"

"No! If I were to kill you, I would be no better than you!"

"Ah! So, this is why Libran chose you. You're as great an idiot as Bran was before you. But not half the hero. Pray to your false gods now, little prince; for now, you die."

The Wanderer struck down at Joryn, who raised his shield to block the blow. "You have the weapons, but you lack the skill," the Wanderer raged. He struck down again, hitting Joryn's left arm with the head of his staff.

Joryn cried out in agony from the searing blow. His arm went numb, as if bitten by a venomous serpent. The shield fell from his grasp, hitting the metal floor with a clang, but still he pressed on.

The Wanderer raised his staff to block a blow from Joryn's sword that had been intended to wound rather than kill. "Your refusal to strike a killing blow is your greatest weakness. If you are unwilling to use equal force to defeat me, you *will* fall before me." He kicked the Shield of Libran out through the still open hatch.

Joryn watched the magical shield's departure with horror. Remaining focused in spite of the loss, he blocked another blow from the Wanderer's poisonous staff. "I've defeated greater enemies than you without taking a single life."

Again, the villain laughed. "Such arrogance! Even the last hero to wield that sword had never faced anything as mighty as *I*!"

Parrying another blow, sweat drenching his pale face, as his only working arm began to tire in spite of the adrenaline, Joryn spat out the words, "You *aren't* the Wanderer!"

The villain, no longer laughing, silently bombarded the young prince with blow after blow against the hated Sword of Libran. The lettering of the ancient words carved into its pitch-black blade began to glow white with the sword's inner power, but the Wanderer would not have it. Not from this upstart prince who didn't even *understand* the weapons that he wielded. Finally, he struck Joryn's wrist with the central head of his staff, breaking bone. Crying out in pain, Joryn dropped the sword, and the Wanderer watched as it slid across the floor and out through the hatch.

At the unintended loss of the sword, the Wanderer roared out in anger and threw aside his staff.

Unarmed and helpless, Joryn wondered with dread what was to come next, knowing that he had failed in his mission; that he had failed everyone who had ever believed in him—and he had failed none so terribly as he had failed Captain Starro and Willowyll.

The answer came when the enraged Wanderer punched him with all of his might across the face, again and again, then abruptly grabbed him by the collar and leaned in close. "Any in Nod could tell you the story of 'The Legend of Bran,' who made that sword a thorn in my side for years! But after this moment, the moment in which you die, none will ever speak of 'The Legend of Prince Joryn.' You will be a mere footnote in history. The *boy* who failed as the chosen of Libran. You will be forgotten, and all of Nod's creatures will lose hope as the world falls to me! Now look, upstart! Look into my eyes and see the terror of what lies beyond! See what became of your legendary Palo. Look into the very heart of darkness and despair!"

The Wanderer pulled Joryn closer still, and Joryn was forced to look directly into the terrible mask, directly into the shadows that had hidden the Wanderer's eyes from view. Only, as he gazed into that terrible visage, it became instantly clear that there *were* no eyes hidden within. There was only darkness. An absence of light so profound that Joryn's skin went whiter than snow; his entire body colder than death. He could not tear his eyes away from the blackness within the Wanderer's mask; the endless depths of it; the utter hopelessness of the vision of nothingness within that terrible void. And he knew then, all too late, that this was indeed the Wanderer.

And the Wanderer had killed him.

The horror of the moment seemed to last for eons, and Joryn at last cried out in unbridled terror at the hopelessness and emptiness that had pierced his very soul.

At last, the Wanderer let forth a final, mirthless laugh and simply tossed the prince out through the open hatch, into the winds that would carry him to his doom on the merciless rocks far below.

Joryn watched the air ship speed away, as he fell helplessly through the atmosphere. He tried to shake the vision of nothingness from his mind, but he could not, and there seemed no point to even trying.

The Shield of Libran flew up beneath him unexpectedly, and he absently took hold of the underside straps, despite the pain of his broken wrist. Then it dawned on him. "You … came back for me?"

He began to feel some measure of strength returning to him at the touch of the shield; his mind began to focus. He took in the situation. *I am falling from ten thousand feet … with a shield. I'm still going to die.*

He looked into the distance and saw a Fighter Disc approaching, black smoke billowing from the places where it had been hit by enemy fire. "Hang on, Shield. This … is gonna … hurt."

The Fighter Disc flew beneath him, and Joryn hit the roof of the craft with the full force of his speed. He had two realizations before he lost consciousness. The first was that the shield had taken the brunt of the impact. The second, astoundingly, was that he was somehow still capable of realizing things.

Chapter 10:
Broken Bones, Broken Hearts

By evening, the Fighter Discs and the Imperial Guard had cleaned up all of the remaining robot soldiers, Warclaw and Dreadfin were locked securely away in the palace dungeon, communications between the kingdoms and territories of Nod had been largely restored, and people all across the Empire were beginning to rebuild. But in the wake of the Wanderer's terror, there remained many things that could never be restored.

Kail and his wife Maressah approached Willowyll's quarters, hand in hand, only to be stopped by a guard. "I'm sorry, Your Highnesses, but Princess Willowyll is not to be disturbed."

"I'm afraid I must see her anyway, Janzo," Kail said. "She is my sister, and she is suffering."

Tears in his own eyes, Janzo said, "She is in agony, my prince. She has told me to make no exceptions. She wishes solitude."

"Lieutenant Janzo," Maressah said solemnly, "I will take full responsibility for your defiance, when you let us through."

" 'When?' "

"That's right, because Kail and I are going to see Willowyll, right now."

"But—"

"Oh, what're you gonna do, Janzo? Shoot me?" Princess Maressah walked boldly past the guard and on towards the door, which she opened gingerly.

Kail shrugged and patted the guardsman on the shoulder. "That's why I love her." He smiled sadly. "Stay here all night, Janzo. I want to know when she's inconsolable. I want to know when she needs my shoulder to cry on."

Janzo nodded. "She needs it now, my prince."

Kail nodded and joined his wife at the door. They cautiously walked in and found Willowyll seated on the side of her bed, staring out the window into the darkness of the night in silence. She turned and took in the sight of her brother and sister-in-law, reddened eyes filled with tears. She tried to put on a strong face, but her lips began to tremble, the tears began to fall, and she could hold her sobs in no more, as Kail and Maressah went to her, sitting on either side of her, and holding her as she wailed aloud, giving wordless voice to the grieving of her broken heart.

They held her in their arms, until her tears ran dry.

***

A week later, to the day, Miiko Quickwing and Dorran Equus stepped into the infirmary, not knowing what to expect. When Joryn smiled at them from his bed, through all of his cuts and slowly fading bruises, they both smiled back in relief.

"About time you woke up!" Equus said in his booming voice.

"Absolutely *everyone* wants to see you," Quickwing added. "We are honored to be the first."

Joryn nodded. "The doctors tell me it was pretty touch and go. They tell me Kabed saved me. But there's more to it than that. So much more. Has there been any word from the Wanderer since I've been out?"

"None," Dorran said. "The coward is hiding away, licking his wounds."

"If he even *was* the Wanderer," Quickwing added.

Joryn's demeanor changed then. "He *is* the Wanderer, and I'm afraid I left him without any wounds to lick. I failed." He shook his head and said again, more softly, "I failed." He looked to them, poignantly. "And Starro …"

"I knew the captain well," Dorran said. "He went with you, because he believed it was the right course of action. And it *was*. That terrorist monster escaped us, true, but because of you and Starro, we know we did *everything* in our power to capture him before he did."

"That's just the thing, though, Dorran. Everything in our power … it wasn't enough. It won't be enough when he comes for us again. And he will. I tell you, I *know* he is the Wanderer." Haunted, he told them, "I looked into his eyes. He isn't … of this world." He looked to his bedside, where the Shield of Libran rested against the wall. "And I lost the sword," he said, distantly.

"Perhaps you did," Quickwing said with a grin. "But I found it." He unsheathed the sword at his side and presented it to Joryn.

Amazed, Joryn took the sword in both hands, as his sword arm remained encumbered with a cast to mend his broken wrist. A surge of warmth coursed through him at the touch of the ancient weapon. "Miiko! How?" Joryn looked the shining, miraculously undamaged blade over in his hands, feeling as though he'd been reunited with a long-lost friend.

"As of this morning, my wounds were healed enough, so I went flying, near the place where you fell, and … It sounds strange, but it's almost as though the sword *wanted* to be found. I saw it glistening, but it wasn't the normal gleam of a sword. It was the writing inscribed on it. It was lighting up, and that's what got my attention. So, I retrieved it and have since been its devoted guardian, awaiting your return."

"It *did* call out to you, Miiko. I think the sword and shield … I think they're alive."

Quickwing and Dorran exchanged a look.

Joryn smirked. "I know how it sounds. I have much to tell all of you. I saw so many strange things on the day of the battle. Some of them wonderful, but most … absolutely terrible." He looked to the Celestian. "But I am grateful to you, Miiko. The doctors told me what you did. How you saved the palace. I knew you had it in you. One thing I learned was that I never need worry about the palace when my friends are here. This palace is indeed full of heroes."

"I would never have been able without your belief in me, Joryn," Quickwing said. "I would have let my handicap defeat me without the Wanderer even raising a hand."

Joryn winced at the memory of the Wanderer raising a hand; slapping the gun from Starro; punching Joryn in the face; pulling him close …

"My prince?" Dorran asked, concerned. "Are you all right?"

Joryn looked back to the two warriors. "I called you both here for a reason." He laid the sword down beside him in the little bed. "I want you to train me."

Again, the two heroes exchanged a confused look.

"In what respect?" Dorran asked.

"And far be it from us to belittle your command in—"

"No, not at all," Joryn cut the Celestian off. "I know, I am your leader, but the reality is that I have minimal skill in combat. I have been given this sword and shield, but I am not a master of either. I am not a master of warfare. I am not a warrior at all. I am a prince. The youngest prince. Most babied of all my brothers and sisters. Perhaps most spoiled and pampered by the eleven of them *and* by my teachers. I charmed my way into an alliance with the dragons of Din. I got lucky in Chiroptera. The Wanderer is a very real threat. I can't *talk* a bomb out of exploding in the palace, and …" Before continuing, he took a moment to fight back tears of grief, then at last, he said the words that had threatened to overwhelm him, "I can't *charm* Captain Starro back to life. And no amount of *luck* is going to end the Wanderer's threat to our world.

"I stand by my resolve, never to take a life. But I fought the Wanderer, and he defeated me soundly. Illium and I faced his agent, Warclaw, three times, and *twice* met with utter defeat. The fact is: if I *am* to be your leader, if I am to be the *champion* of Libran, as neither friends nor enemies will ever let me forget, then I must be *better.* I must be a *master* swordsman, like you, Miiko. And I must be a *master* at hand-to-hand combat, like you, Dorran. So, I ask you, with the deepest respect, please, train me, and do not hold back because of my title or my perceived innocence. Train me as you would train the lowest of your students, so that I may, under your guidance, become the finest."

"It would be the *greatest* honor, Joryn," Miiko said with a bow.

"Not to mention fun," Dorran said, nudging the Celestian playfully. "Get ready for sheer hell, boy!" He laughed. "The bruises you've got now are nothing."

Joryn smiled, though his eyes told the tale of his unyielding sorrow.

Just then, Golan Binju appeared on the wall screen in front of Joryn's bed. "My prince, it's good to see you awake."

"Thanks, Golan."

"I know the doctors don't want you to be disturbed, but there is a call for you, and I thought you would want to take it. It's from the Whispering Plains."

"Of course I'll take it! Thank you, Golan."

"We'll take our leave," Miiko said. "We have a training regimen to prepare."

"That we do," Dorran agreed. "Enjoy your rest, while you can."

The pair left, and Joryn answered the call to see the face of his beloved Galen.

"Thank the gods you're alive!" Galen said, a weight visibly lifting from his countenance.

Joryn smiled. "I have to agree with that sentiment. And you. The doctors told me that you were okay; that you were managing the governance for your father. I'm so sorry, Galen. I wish I could have been there."

"I'd say your hands were pretty full at the time. I guess I'll let you off the hook. Besides, *I* was there, so no further heroics required, right?"

"Right."

"So, how are you, *really*?" Galen asked. "Please tell me there's something I can do."

"Just caring enough to ask will do for now," Joryn assured him. "Between the doctors and Tianna, I'm sure they'll have me healed up and running again in no time. What about you? How are *you* really?"

Galen looked down for a moment, then met Joryn's eyes again. "It's hard. I'm not ready to lose my father. I'm not ready … to grow up. I know, I'm twenty. I'm a grown man. But it's strange. Losing a parent, the idea of it, is like losing permission to be vulnerable. It's like losing the right to be seen as a child, or to feel like one. It's something I didn't realize was there to be lost. And that child within me still needs his father and mother. At least, I think I do. And I'm not ready to let go of that need. And my cousin; he's like a brother to me. I don't know what I'll do if I lose either one of them. I don't know what I'll do at all." His demeanor changed ever so slightly. "It makes me angry. If I ever find out who let that Brother Clock *thing* into my father's court …"

He let the thought trail off, as he met Joryn's gaze; the fires of outrage and incredulity painting his expression. "Can you believe he just *ran away* like that? The monster had us right where he wanted us. We were crippled. The entire Empire. He *held* the Imperial palace! All that power … and he just ran away. It doesn't make sense."

Joryn considered that, thinking back on all the doctors had told him about the manner in which the villain had taken Palace Nod. "Maybe it does," he said at last. "He's a powerful enemy, but he's also a coward. He sent those clockwork men to bomb our capitals. He sent his lieutenants to take the palace. He only arrived on the scene after it was done. He may have planned the assault, but he had no intention of facing anyone in combat himself. When the tide turned, he knew he'd be our primary target. He wasn't willing to wait around and see just how many of our seasoned warriors would attack him all at once." His mind flashed back to his defeat aboard the *Darkstar*, the horrific death of Captain Starro. "Not that it would have made any difference." He shook his head, frustrated. "Maybe it *doesn't* make sense. Or, maybe," he realized, "he was afraid of something else. Something we don't even know about."

"He's a fool," Galen said.

Haunted, Joryn nodded. "Or very clever." He thought again of the battle on the *Darkstar*, wincing at the relentless memory of Starro's death, his wrist aching in pain as he recalled the bone-breaking blow from the Wanderer's venomous staff. "He knows what we're made of now. Next time, he'll compensate."

"Do you think it was really him? The Wanderer?" Galen asked.

Joryn tried and failed to block the memory of looking into the empty darkness that was the face of the Wanderer; the coldness of death itself, the absence of light and hope. With a distant look, he answered, "Yes. I am certain of it, and he is the greatest threat that Nod has ever known."

"Joryn … Whatever he did to you …" Galen looked down again. "I wish I could be there with you."

A rebellious smile curling his lips, Joryn countered, "I wish I could be *there* with you. And I will be, when I'm able."

Galen pondered Joryn's words. "The Wanderer. The myth come to life."

"I wonder," Joryn said, again sounding distant, "if *this* is the reason that Libran picked now, after three thousand years, to call a new champion to carry his sword and shield. I've wondered, 'Why now?' for some time. I've wondered, 'Why now, and why me?' I know the sword and shield are only symbols, not meant to kill. But why bring those symbols back at this specific point in time?"

"If the Wanderer's return *is* the reason that Libran picked now," Galen said, "then the Sword and Shield are more than just symbols. And you *are* the perfect choice to bear them. You're the only one who could use their very symbolism as a weapon, and Libran knows that. That's why he chose you. If this is the case, then you were chosen to defeat the Wanderer in this age, just as Bran did millennia ago." He paused, considering, then looked his lover in the eyes with deep concern. "Joryn, this changes everything."

The saga of *The Sword of Libran* will continue,
with Book IV:
The Mech Valley Debacle

About the Author

Glenn Slade Clark, Jr. is the author of nine books, including the novel *Cry, Wolf: Shadow of the Werewolf*, the short fiction anthology *The Great Debate*, the Gothic horror series *The Chronicles of Nightfire, Texas*, and two fantasy series: *Metrognomes* and *The Legends of Nod.* He lives in Dallas, Texas, where he is currently hard at work on the next adventure in *The Legends of Nod.*

www.GlennSladeClarkJr.com

www.ingramcontent.com/pod-product-compliance
Lightning Source LLC
LaVergne TN
LVHW010623100826
845148LV00014B/3082

* 9 7 8 1 6 1 8 1 5 1 1 9 3 *